ALSO BY
SIRI CALDWELL

MISTLETOE MISHAP

DEAL-BREAKER

Angels

ANGEL'S TOUCH

EARTH ANGEL

THE
MERMAID
HYPOTHESIS

Brussels Sprout Press
P.O. Box 42133
Arlington, VA 22204
United States of America

First edition: October 2022

THE
MERMAID
HYPOTHESIS

SIRI CALDWELL

1

There was a fine line between confidence and recklessness, and Niua knew precisely where it was. Boarding a ship in a desolate stretch of ocean might not be the safest thing she'd ever done, but she was good at not getting caught.

Far above her, where sunlight reached, a carousel of bottles dangling from a thick steel cable was lowered over the side of the ship. Down it plummeted, into the sea's frigid depths, down to where Niua waited, then sinking past her, toward the abyss.

She waited. She was good at waiting.

She'd observed this type of ship often enough to know it was a research vessel. The contraption was some type of scientific instrument, and the bottles weren't on a one-way trip. The instrument slowed. Stopped. Reversed course.

She wrapped long strands of kelp decoratively around her waist, adjusted the gold bracelet that coiled up her forearm like a serpent, and kept an eye on that cable. On its way up, she intercepted it and clambered onto the metal frame. She settled at the top with her tail curled around a beam and her arms wrapped around the cable for balance. As they rose, the bottles beneath her clanged shut in sequence, each one at a progressively shallower depth, collecting water samples. Soon the ship's hull loomed ominously close, a dark shadow obstructing the sunlight. With a thought, she transformed the seaweed she'd draped around her body into a greenish brown dress that clung flatteringly to her curves. Her tail released its hold as her hands tightened their grip. Muscles cramped deep in her core. She braced herself against a tingling shudder of nausea—and a spike of excitement—and when she looked down, her tail was gone, and she had legs.

∞

Seawater sluiced down her face as she broke the surface. Fresh air rushed into her lungs. The instrument swung toward the wide deck of the ship. The crewman operating the winch yelled something unintelligible. The carousel hit the deck, bottles clanging. The impact jostled her hard, nearly throwing her off. She squeezed the shuddering cable and held on.

Of course the man saw her.

But he didn't know what he was seeing. People saw what they expected to see, and nowadays no one expected to see a mermaid.

Niua rubbed her face against her biceps to push her long, wet hair out of her eyes.

The man rushed toward her, gesturing wildly and still shouting, but the hum of the ship's engine made it impossible to make out the words until he was directly in front of her.

Not an issue. They didn't need to speak for this part.

"What the…?" He unlatched one of the bottles and hauled it off the carousel, using his whole body to handle the weight. "They're going to kill you if you contaminated the CTD." He unlatched the next bottle.

These water samples were more important than her mysterious arrival? Surprising, but not insurmountable. Niua scooted to the edge of the frame and carefully slid off, not ready to test her uncertain legs with a jump.

Her bare feet touched hot metal where the winch was bolted to the deck. She flinched and hopped away onto damp wooden planks. Better. She smoothed her dress and blinked water from her eyes.

"I thought for sure you'd ask how I fell overboard," she said in a sultry voice, pitching it so he'd strain to hear. So he'd *want* to hear. So he'd look.

The poor helpless creature. Once he looked her in the eye, he'd be hers.

She twisted a lock of her dripping hair around her finger and gazed at him from underneath her lashes.

She hated doing this.

Couldn't be helped, though.

"You…what? You…fell? Overboard? Lucky you caught the cable. Damn lucky. But…how…?" His gaze darted to the sea, to the bottles, to her.

Eye contact. *Yes.*

He fumbled the heavy bottle in his arms and caught it before he dropped it, never looking away.

She could gush about how heroic he was to have rescued her, but no. She preferred to save the dramatics for emergencies. Instead, she eased into a slow, shy smile. "I wasn't ready for a watery grave."

The harsh lines in the man's grimy, weather-beaten face relaxed. Some women—those who cared about such things—might have found him attractive in his hardhat and orange coveralls, called him ruggedly handsome. To her, his looks were irrelevant.

"Don't recognize you," he said.

"No?" She held his gaze until he nodded like everything he'd ever puzzled over was starting to make sense.

"Er…don't know that I've met all the scientists, of course."

"Of course." If this explanation made sense to him, she was delighted to go along with it. "You've been occupied with your work. No time to socialize."

He nodded again.

Men were so easy. With her goddess-given magic, it wasn't even a challenge. Sometimes they fought it, but most men were like this one, willing to believe whatever she told them. Eager to forget she didn't belong among them. Willing to believe she was harmless—as long as she had legs. Once they discovered the truth, things didn't go so well for her kind.

She wouldn't let that happen, though. She had no intention of getting herself killed.

"I need you to show me where the charts are kept."

He looked at her blankly.

"Nautical charts? Maps? The images you're drawing of the seafloor."

Nothing.

"Using air guns?"

Just how hard had she whammied him?

She gentled her voice. "*Ping*?"

These ships were always making noise. *Ping ping ping.* Out and back and out and back they went, traveling in a pattern of evenly spaced lines, firing bursts of sound to map the ocean floor. *Boom boom boom* like thoughtless noisy neighbors, vibrating the back of her skull and making her head pound. Searching for oil, usually, although their reasons made no difference. It was modern man's equivalent of the way she bounced her own high-frequency screeches off her surroundings to create mental images when she navigated in the darkness of the deep, where sunlight couldn't reach and eyes were useless.

His face cleared. "You mean the swath mapping? The sonar?"

"Yes." Finally.

"I'll walk you over to the geophysicists. They'll know."

"I'm sure they will." She smiled encouragingly and cocked her head in the direction of the interior, indicating he should lead the way.

He blinked.

Oh dear.

Niua eased around him and made for the door. At this point, turning her back on him and breaking eye contact would not tone down her magic's effect, not significantly. If she was lucky, it would be just enough that when it was time for her to leave, he wouldn't throw himself overboard in pursuit. She didn't need another death on her conscience.

She glanced over her shoulder to confirm he was following her and not glued to the deck in a mindless daze. "Coming?"

∞

The geophysics lab—as Courtland, the winch operator who believed he'd rescued her, referred to it—featured a bank of computer monitors bolted to the bulkhead on metal scaffolding, three monitors high and five across, each displaying a different graph or image that flickered with incoming data, subtly changing with each passing minute.

The space was packed with men, most of them arguing about something scientific, shouting over each other to be heard over the whirring and clanging of the ship's engine somewhere in the bowels of the ship. Two men ignored the commotion, too intent on their work to be drawn in. No one seemed to notice her arrival or pay any attention to the lone unoccupied seat that slid across the deck with the rolling of the ship, merely pushing it aside blindly when it bumped into them.

Niua's vision blurred. The cacophony and the claustrophobic, nervy energy of so many people in a tight space were difficult to adjust to. They always were. No matter where she found herself when the earth and the moon and the sun returned to this point in their cycle, the transition to the world of land-dwellers was always jarring. She gazed unseeingly at the solid bulkhead as if she could echolocate through it to the ocean and find the distant horizon to steady herself.

"Here we are," Courtland said. "Science Central."

Niua blinked. She could do this. She had to. She'd been part of humanity once. No human environment was truly alien to her.

"This what you need?" Courtland asked.

Was it? She didn't see any charts lying about, but there were plenty of sailors here who could help. She nodded her thanks, then turned to the man seated nearest to her and tapped him on the shoulder.

He looked up and scowled, clearly irritated at the interruption. "Can I help you?"

"I certainly hope so." She held his gaze and swayed subtly

toward him, relaxing into the ship's motion. "May I see the charts?"

"Charts?" The man blinked as if she'd spoken in a foreign tongue.

She smoothed her hands down her hips. Had she inadvertently slipped into another language? "To show what's down there beneath the waves?" *And save me years of searching on my own? When your ship moves so much faster than I can swim?*

"Ah. Yes." He smiled in the relaxed manner of a man securely under her spell and turned toward the screens. "What you're seeing here is the real-time feed from the..."

Niua's mind stumbled over the unfamiliar vocabulary as she strained to follow his explanation.

"You're..." She watched closely as he babbled on and pointed to something on one of the monitors. *This* was his chart? On a screen?

"...color-coded..."

Yes, she could see how color was being used to indicate depth. That much was obvious.

"...as the acoustical signals bounce back..."

Of course she understood the concept of sonar. What did he take her for?

"...high-resolution bathymetry..."

"But..." She covered her mouth in dismay. They were doing it all on machines? How was she going to search a machine? She knew how to riffle through a drawer full of nautical charts. Paper charts. She didn't know how to use a *machine*. Not these machines. These computers. She'd watched the gadgets proliferate to every size boat and every shore, but watching from afar hadn't taught her how to use them.

A sensible navigator would keep paper on hand for backup in case of electrical failure, but this sonar wasn't for navigation. It was for exploration. They were sailing in uncharted waters. They were in the blank spaces where cartographers used to draw sea monsters to obscure the fact they knew virtually nothing of what lay in the ocean's depths.

Exactly where she wanted to be.

Well. There was no reason she couldn't sit with this man and have him show her the images. It would take hours, and she'd have to stay alert to all the men who saw or overheard them, casting her spell on them if they tried to intervene, but it could be done. It felt more exposed and more dangerous than searching an empty stateroom, but this was why she had legs: to move among humans as one of them and not have to hide.

"Spotted any shipwrecks?" she asked.

The man laughed like it was a joke. "Hunting for sunken treasure would be fun, but we're doing science here."

Niua placed her palms on his shoulders and leaned down until her head was level with his. "But one might stumble across a wreck by chance, *n'est-ce pas*? In the process of doing"—her lips were close enough that he'd feel her breath on the back of his neck—"science?"

"Yes. I mean, no. I mean, it's…"

Poor man. She did feel a little bad about this.

And about Courtland as well. Her delightful winch operator-turned-guide remained close at hand, ready to offer assistance should she tire of this man monitoring the sonar, blissfully unaware she would do nothing but disappoint him.

"It's possible we could come across a shipwreck," the geophysicist explained, clearly wanting to make her happy. "But we haven't."

"Nothing at all?" She hadn't visited this part of the world in ages, but where there were submerged hazards and violent storms, wrecks were sure to be found.

Sailors used to say she and her sisters were to blame for those losses, but modern thinking had evolved. Take that incident just a few years ago, before she'd left her usual haunts in the North Sea to travel halfway around the world. She'd spied a tour guide leading vacationing divers to the wreck of a once-beautiful sailing ship, its prow buried in centuries of sand. According to the authoritative voice that carried across the waves, the ship had been blown off course during a squall and had struck an unseen sand bar and foundered due to what the guide referred to as *navigator error.*

The navigator had made an error, all right. Imagining she'd be interested in having sex with him on the deck of his ship had clearly been an error.

A fatal one.

Not that she'd meant to destroy his vessel. All she'd meant to do was warn him about that sand bar. It wasn't her fault he couldn't keep his eyes on where he was going.

Niua leaned a smidge closer. The man at the computer breathed faster.

"I could suggest we change course for an area with more underwater hazards, where someone would've been likely to wreck," he offered.

"A pirate, for example?"

"Sure," he said. "Pirates. Why not."

"What the—" a female voice behind them sputtered. "What do you mean, change course?"

Niua whirled around. With all the noise, she hadn't heard anyone approach. Her arms flew up defensively.

The woman made a startled jump.

A woman aboard. Just her luck.

There'd been a time when women weren't allowed to set foot on seafaring vessels because they were believed to bring bad luck. It was heartening to know the superstition had faded, but at the moment it was a tad inconvenient.

The woman's glare wasn't directed at her, though. Not yet. "Hudson?"

"Calm down, Mallory," said Niua's besotted geophysicist. Hudson, apparently.

A triangular pendant dangled from a leather cord at the woman's—Mallory's—neck, nestled in the vee of her button-down shirt and disappearing into her cleavage. Not a harmless seashell or a dainty jeweled starfish or a polished chip of sea glass. A shark's tooth. Pretty sure. Niua had sharp vision and she could certainly recognize a shark's tooth when she saw one.

Mallory looked Niua up and down. Her chest rose and fell with powerful breaths, causing the shark's tooth to sink deeper into hiding. She frowned at Niua's bare feet.

Oops.

Footwear was always the hardest item of clothing to find when she came ashore. She hadn't even bothered asking Courtland for a spare pair of work boots since they would never have fit.

Mallory's gaze snapped up from Niua's feet. "Who are you?"

"She's one of yours," Courtland said, stepping to Niua's side as if to defend her and clamping a supportive hand on her elbow. Because ships weren't claustrophobic enough already. "A member of the science team."

Mallory's jaw tightened with a level of intensity that did not bode well. "Is that what she told you?"

Well, no, not precisely. Niua had simply encouraged him to assume whatever made sense.

She could tell Mallory wasn't fooled. Niua knew how these ships worked, though. There were passengers, and there were crew. Here, the passengers were the scientists, so…

"I work in the engine room," Niua said. That location had to be sufficiently out of the way. None of the scientists would venture belowdecks into that noisy hell if they didn't need to, and Courtland would back her up no matter what she said. "Right, Courtland?"

"Right," he said.

"Nice try." Mallory's gaze fell to Courtland's hand on Niua's elbow. "Who is she, Courtland?"

"I…er…um…"

The poor guy knew perfectly well that Niua was not one of his crewmates, but Niua wasn't worried. He wouldn't say anything.

"Never mind." Mallory turned her attention back to Niua. "I don't know what's going on here, but I'm going to take a wild guess and assume you don't work in the engine room. So. What are you doing aboard this ship? And what are you doing this close to our computers?"

"Relax," Hudson said. Because that was sure to defuse the situation. "She's harmless."

"She's not supposed to be here," Mallory said. "Or seeing our data."

Hudson snorted and shook his head. "You think she's committing academic espionage?"

"It's a possibility."

He made another rude noise. "It really isn't."

"I've met every single person on this ship. She's not on the passenger list as either scientist or crew."

"Who memorizes the passenger manifest?" grumbled someone else.

Mallory didn't back down. "All of you think this is perfectly normal. To be four days from shore and find a stranger aboard."

Another man with a brash, abrasive voice said, "Don't be so paranoid."

This was getting out of hand. Niua noted the man who'd made that comment and narrowed her eyes. It was nice of him to defend an innocent-looking stranger, but really.

Mallory crossed her arms. "Research vessels don't have stowaways. The captain is going to flip."

"The *captain*?" snickered another one of the men. "That's who's going to?"

Mallory ignored him and took another hard look at what Niua was wearing. "Why are your clothes wet?"

Leave it to the one woman in the group to be the only one to notice that detail.

"I…" Niua hesitated. Courtland had believed her when she told him she'd fallen overboard, but Courtland wasn't currently in control of his powers of reasoning. She had a feeling Mallory would be harder to convince. "I…"

"Where did you come from?" Mallory's voice rose. She turned to the others. "Does anyone know how she got here?"

"She…swam?" Courtland said.

Niua was beginning to feel a bit too much like a lobster on the verge of being thrown into a pot of boiling water. She swept her hair off her shoulders and gathered it at the back of her neck, flared her elbows on either side of her face, and shot Mallory a smoldering look.

Mallory slowly shook her head like her day could not get any worse.

Niua flushed with embarrassment at what Mallory must think of her. She dropped her arms to her sides. Why had she done that? She knew better than that—women never succumbed to her magic. It simply didn't work on them.

If she wanted to seduce this woman—and part of her did, for reasons that had nothing to do with bathymetric data and everything to do with the fact that Mallory was the only one making an effort to protect her ship—because there was something noble about that, and Niua had always had a weakness for women who took their responsibilities seriously—*if* she wanted to seduce her, she'd have to do it the hard way. The non-magical way. The way she had no time for.

"Swam." Mallory's voice was soft, which was somehow worse than when she'd been loud. "Really, Courtland? She swam? From where? We're in the middle of the ocean. No way could anyone swim."

Oh dear. Time to go. Mallory was thinking far too clearly, and there were too many people here, and crowds were good at overpowering creatures who didn't belong.

Niua pushed past them toward the exit and bolted.

2

Once every eighteen years, Niua ventured ashore.

For the past two weeks, she'd watched the moon wax larger and larger and known it was almost time. She'd felt it: The jitteriness. The ache in her tail. The feeling that her skin was too tight, warning her that when the full moon arrived, she'd be able to emerge from the sea and live on two legs—while counting the days and making sure she returned before the next full moon, because if she didn't, she'd die.

Mere hours ago, she'd been drifting beneath the surface of the sea, spiraling with anticipation, gazing upward at the moonlight spearing through the blackness, wavering and distorted, telling her the time had come.

And now her body, so powerful in its natural environment, had forgotten how to run.

She stumbled through the ship and across the open deck on her bare feet as boots pounded some distance behind her, clearly in pursuit. She hurtled over a coil of heavy chain toward freedom. Her toes caught on a link. She tripped, cursing her lack of coordination. She knew how to do this. She wasn't a seal who couldn't do anything but flop around on her belly. She was acting like one now, though, rolling off the obstacle instead of righting herself and using her legs.

"What are you doing?" shouted a female voice. She sounded close.

Niua scrambled to her feet. Almost there. She reached the bulwark and swung one leg over the wet guardrail, hooking it with her knee. The ship heaved. Sea spray hit her face. She hoisted herself up.

Strong arms grabbed her by the waist.

Feminine arms.

Mallory.

Niua screamed.

No. She kicked behind her, but with Mallory pressed to her back and the bulwark in the way, she didn't have the space to kick hard.

"Let me go!"

Mallory tightened her hold and Niua clamped her elbows around the slippery rail, resisting with all her strength, straining toward the waves. It was instinct, and it overrode everything.

"Stop," Mallory said, her voice low and controlled and too close to her ear to be anything but dangerous.

It shouldn't have, but even as Niua fought her, something in that voice seeped past her defenses and calmed her, just a little, just enough so she could think. Think, rather than panic. She was trapped, but she wasn't caged. She wasn't injured. She would be able to free herself.

Niua eased up on her grip. Slightly.

Think.

She had options. She looked human. No one knew what she was. All she had to do was be patient, and stop flailing like a fish caught in a net, and not act suspicious, and she'd get another opportunity to escape. She was not going to die. Not today.

Mallory hauled her backward, away from the edge, and Niua allowed it, making herself go limp. Her leg slid off the guardrail; her foot hit the deck. At this point her chances of finding the leverage to throw herself forward and over the side were low. And she'd prefer not to take anyone with her into the sea. Humans tended not to survive that.

"Let go," Niua tried again, meekly, like she was on the verge of defeat.

Mallory's arms stayed locked around her waist. "No one's committing suicide on my watch."

What? Oh. Of course she'd think… Oh.

Niua could hear other people closing in. She turned her head to look over Mallory's shoulder. Several of the men from earlier had followed them onto the deck. Them, she could handle. Mallory was the real threat, obviously quick enough and strong enough and clearheaded enough to catch her if she released her and Niua tried to make another run for it.

"I'm not comm—"

"Sharkette would rather kill you herself," said one of the men.

Niua tensed. She was reasonably sure it was a joke, but…

The bulwark was so close. The sea stretched out into infinity, calling to her, singing its beautiful, seductive song, promising safety.

"Don't you dare try it," Mallory warned.

Niua startled, surprised Mallory had correctly read her intention. It had certainly been a long time since she'd had any real human interaction, though, so perhaps Mallory's powers of observation were nothing unusual.

"You almost sound like you care about me," Niua said, purposely relaxing into Mallory's body, intending to sink into her chest and distract her with a seductive wiggle.

Instead, Mallory blocked, and Niua collided with her shoulder and hip. Because Niua was an idiot who needed to be reminded her usual tactics didn't work on this woman.

Mallory didn't let go. "You're going inside, and you're talking to the captain."

"All right," Niua agreed. Or perhaps lied.

Mallory scowled like she didn't trust her. Intelligent woman.

"I'll take her," offered a man with a goatee.

"No. I'll do it," said another man.

"What's going on?" asked someone else.

"Didn't you see her?" the goateed one said. "She was climbing over the rail."

"What?"

"Yeah. And we don't have time to waste rescuing her drowning ass. I waited years to get research time on this ship. I'm not pissing away a single minute of it for someone else's bad judgment." He stole Niua from Mallory's hold and yanked her in the direction of the nearest door.

Niua resisted, dropping her weight into her hips to make herself deadweight. She was not in the mood to allow herself to be dragged to see the captain.

"She stronger than you?" razzed a guy who wore the same protective coveralls Courtland did and carried himself like he was used to hauling heavy fishing lines. "Need help?"

Niua twisted away from the would-be assistant. He caught one of her arms anyway.

Fine. She turned to her first captor, the impatient goateed one, and stared deep into his eyes. She focused on the power inside her heart and felt it stir. "There's really no need to restrain me," she told him, anchoring herself in the knowledge of who she was and waiting for him to relax his grip. It didn't take long.

She turned to the guard in coveralls and locked eyes with him next. Her heart swelled with magic. "I'm not going anywhere."

He nodded, looking dazed, and released her.

"What are you…?" Mallory looked disbelievingly at the three of them.

Before Niua could decide which way to run, Mallory had seized one of her wrists. Another man, who'd been hanging back and whose gaze she hadn't yet caught, took advantage of the situation to twist her free arm behind her back. Which meant he was standing behind her where she couldn't make good eye contact.

Aargh. Niua jerked in frustration. Why in the goddess's name was she failing so miserably at this?

"Got her," said the new guy. As if Mallory hadn't captured her first.

Mallory focused on Niua and glared straight into her eyes. "I have no idea what you're doing to these guys, but you're not going to bat your eyelashes at me, do you understand? It's not going to work."

"I know." Mallory didn't know just how depressingly right she was.

"And it's not going to work on them, either," Mallory said.

There she was wrong, but Niua didn't bother to correct her.

"Can you loan her your shirt?" Mallory asked the man behind Niua.

His shirt? Niua glanced down and noticed her dress had ripped at the shoulder during the struggle and threatened to expose more than her arm if she continued to fight. She was so used to wearing nothing at all that she hadn't paid attention. As far as she was concerned, clothing was a nuisance that served only one purpose: to avoid attracting undue attention.

"Can't. I'd have to let go of her to take it off."

Mallory turned to the cluster of men watching. "Anyone?"

A man twice Niua's size stripped off his shirt and handed it over.

"Thanks," Mallory said. She nodded at the one who was securing Niua's arm behind her back. "Let go, please."

The man released her. Then Mallory let go as well and helped Niua put her arms into the arm holes, one and then the other, her hands gentle and careful with the shoulder that had been twisted.

Niua stared at her, sure that she was gaping like a fish.

An unattractive fish.

Who ought to be taking advantage of this chance to escape.

Run, she commanded her paralyzed body. *Run!*

Her limbs didn't respond.

Whoever said the body's reaction to adrenaline was *fight or flight* didn't have the self-awareness to admit the truth: it was *fight or flight or play dead.*

She hated playing dead.

Mallory closed the buttons one by one, her fingers efficient and determined, her annoyance seeming to fade and her face softening into an expression that looked like compassion.

For a moment, Niua remembered what it felt like to be cared for, and she forgot about wanting to run.

She could stay.

A day.

Or two.

Try again to get the information she needed.

Spend time around someone she couldn't manipulate, someone who reminded her how it felt to interact with others instead of watching from afar. It had been so long since anyone had talked to her, or touched her, or even known she existed, and it was so, *so* tempting to reach for the promise of connection and not let go.

Mallory rolled up the shirt's too-long sleeves as if Niua couldn't do it herself, and Niua let her, too stunned to resist.

"We're going inside," Mallory said, smoothing the fabric across Niua's shoulders before thinking better of it and jerking her hands away. "Do *not* try anything."

"I wasn't batting my eyelashes at—"

"The captain will decide what to do with you," Mallory said. "You can save your breath for him."

3

There was a fine line between confidence and stupidity, and Mallory wasn't sure which of the two had led her to a career that required her to spend weeks at sea.

She loved being in the water, diving below the waves to where the sea was calm. But topside, at the uneasy interface between air and sea, was a different experience. She didn't know a single marine scientist who hadn't lost their lunch or at least their footing in rough seas—science wasn't performed on gargantuan cruise ships too big for the ocean to wrestle with—but when she had trouble staying upright, it felt like one more way to lose the professional respect of her peers and of the sailors who made these expeditions possible.

So what did she do when she led their suicidal stranger onto the bridge? She stumbled and had to scramble for a bolted-down chair to regain her balance. The Sea Monster's captain, of course, was not squeezing the furniture in a death grip. At least the flirtatious supposed crewmember wasn't any better at staying on her feet than Mallory was. Which was further evidence against her, because no way would a real sailor not have better sea legs.

"Hello, Captain." Mallory did her best to stand tall without letting go of the chair. "Is this woman part of your crew?"

Captain Winata could have answered yes or no. Instead, his posture stiffened, and Mallory remembered the many well-meaning people who had, over the years, warned her to maybe keep her opinions to herself rather than complain too loudly to higher-ups. Twice, she'd chosen to resign rather than watch a project fail because no one dared speak up, or worse, no one listened—not to those without the requisite power and status. She considered it a positive personality trait, even if it hadn't resulted in employers lining up to hire her.

"What's the problem?" the captain said carefully, as if he hadn't yet decided whether to be angry at the interruption or happy to have someone to chat with.

"I think she's a stowaway," Mallory said.

He frowned. "A *what*?"

Yes, she knew how it sounded. They weren't going anywhere but out to sea, then back to the same port they started from. Any stowaway trying to leave the country had picked the wrong ship.

"Or a spy."

The captain put his fingers to his lips like he was fighting a smirk. "Someone wants to steal information on the chemical composition of seawater? Mud? Lava? The location of a coral reef?"

Because my life's work is so boring, you mean?

Mallory stood up straighter and released the chair. "She was interested in the swath scans. Oil companies might—"

"Oil companies conduct their own surveys," he said. "They don't have to resort to sending beautiful young women to sneak aboard my ship."

He had a point. If anyone wanted Mallory's research, they'd hack into her computer once she returned to Australian soil and had transferred her data off the ship.

Why did she even care what this stranger was up to? She didn't. She had work to do. She didn't have time for distractions. Getting time on the *Sea Monster* to test her theories had meant competing against dozens of respected marine geologists and waiting forever for her grant to be approved. Two weeks at sea would generate enough data to keep her and all the other scientists aboard busy for at least a year. *If* they collected it.

Captain Winata turned to the stowaway/spy/probably-not-an-engine-room-crewperson. "What is your name, young lady?"

"I'm Niua."

Mallory gripped the back of the chair again. Forcefully. For balance. Not because she was irritated this woman would answer the captain politely but had run away from *her*. There was nothing to be irritated about, because Mallory had been so agitated when she first laid eyes on her that of course Niua had recoiled.

"Ah." The captain nodded. "You prefer to be on a first-name basis. Then I'll introduce myself by my given name as well." He tapped his chest. "Captain."

Mallory couldn't tell if he was mocking the woman, chastising her, or trying to be funny. Maybe Niua couldn't tell either, because all she did was blink, her expression unchanged.

"Are you a pirate, my dear? Shall I throw you in the brig?"

Niua made a dismissive gesture. "You don't have a brig."

Captain Winata laughed.

It was unbelievable the effect this woman had on men. What was it about her, anyway? She wasn't stop-in-your-tracks attractive. Sure, she flirted shamelessly, but the way she'd charmed the guys who'd caught her earlier? Mallory had never seen two seconds of eye contact work like *that*. These guys were only four days from shore; they weren't desperate. They had girlfriends and wives they were devoted to. They were intensely focused on their jobs. They shouldn't be mesmerized by a...a...*distraction*.

"Lash you to the mast?" the captain suggested.

"You don't have one of those, either," Niua said.

"Mallory, why don't you find our guest a place to sleep. If she's not sleeping in a packing crate, we can hardly call her a stowaway."

"There aren't any spare bunks," Mallory protested. No way were the powers that be leaving an empty bed when there was a waiting list of scientists desperate for the chance to get aboard. She'd heard the crew quarters were also full.

"Find someone who will share, and put her on the opposite shift so they take turns sleeping. If you can't find a scientist to volunteer, ask the crew. It won't be the first time they've had to hot bunk."

Mallory nodded. They'd have to put Niua somewhere, because a detour to return her to dry land was impossible. No matter what happened, she was going to be aboard for the rest of the expedition.

"You're not confining me to a cabin," Niua said.

"Not to worry. I'll find something to keep you occupied," Captain Winata said. "How about swabbing the deck? I've always thought that would be a suitable task for a pirate."

"Swabbing the deck," Niua said, crossing her arms over her chest. What a strange idea. "Why do the undocumented ones always get the cleaning jobs?"

The captain winked at her. His eyes had that clear, farsighted look that men developed from gazing out onto the horizon their whole lives. "Have to make this concerned, security-minded passenger happy and keep a beautiful siren like you away from the scientists."

Niua flinched at the word *siren*.

He didn't mean a real mythical creature. It was a turn of phrase. She covered her reaction by tossing her hair, which was a little over the top even for her. "I wouldn't mind making Mallory happy."

Mallory huffed out a disbelieving breath.

It was no secret that Mallory disapproved of her. If Niua wanted to see that softness in her eyes again, she was going to have to stop defaulting to her natural defense mechanisms and let some of her real personality show.

But at the moment, she needed to focus on the captain, and he would be easier to control if she undid the top buttons of her borrowed shirt. Or positioned her arms strategically lower across her chest to stretch the fabric. Or met his gaze and ensnared him with her magic.

But should she? If she convinced him she should be freed and then immediately jumped overboard, Mallory might not be the only one who'd become suspicious. They wouldn't necessarily guess the truth—since modern men and women believed themselves to be too intelligent to heed their ancestors' fables—but they might watch her, send underwater cameras after her, chase her with far-seeing technology she'd never encountered and didn't understand. She tried to be aware of the ever-changing world as much as she could—particularly the details that affected her own safety—but there were limits to what she could observe from a cautious distance. These researchers could be capable of anything, technology-wise. The only way to be sure she wasn't discovered was to not attract attention.

Unfortunately for her, as a result of her own choices, she was currently the center of attention.

That meant she'd have to blend in and wait until everyone became bored and forgot about her. Then reserve her powers of seduction for the men who operated the sonar machines. That was her real goal: the sonar data. And she still had a good shot at getting it. Her time aboard wouldn't be wasted.

"How close will you get to the atolls to the west?" Niua asked him, avoiding eye contact, since there really was no point. "Or the islands beyond?"

The ship rolled. Mallory was thrown forward. "You've kept track of where we are?"

She looked outraged. It was kind of cute. Kind of made Niua want to kiss the anger right out of her.

The captain let loose a *how-can-you-be-so-daft-you-stupid-landlubber?* sort of snort. "Anyone standing on this bridge could familiarize themselves with our geographic location. It doesn't make her a spy."

Mallory scowled for a fraction of a second before schooling her features into a bland, neutral expression so quickly that if Niua hadn't been paying close attention, she would have missed it.

It was convenient that the captain found Mallory's suspicions unfounded, but he didn't need to laugh at her. How dare he.

Niua had lived a long life. She had lured quite a number of ship's captains to their deaths.

She ignored her unsteady knees and moved into his personal

space, close enough to count the hairs in his bushy eyebrows. She thought about how easy it would be to get revenge…and smiled.

Mallory sucked in a breath. "Don't flirt with him."

"I'm not flirting," Niua said.

"I don't mind," the captain said.

Niua flashed him more teeth.

"He won't fall for it," Mallory said.

"Of course not," Niua agreed pleasantly.

"Everyone on this ship is working twelve-hour days. We don't have time for this. So just…don't." Mallory let go of the chair and tested her balance. "I'll show you to your quarters. You can settle in and start making yourself useful."

Niua winked goodbye to the captain, just to see what Mallory would do.

"You're not *that* sexy," Mallory muttered, stumbling for the exit without checking whether Niua was following her out. The ship rocked and her shoulder hit the bulkhead. "There's got to be someone around here who's immune."

"There is," Niua assured her. "You."

4

With a purposeful stride that left Niua scrambling to keep up, Mallory led the way down three levels to the main cabin deck and down a long, featureless passageway.

"There's no good place to put you," Mallory said. "So you'll have to stay with me."

Not Niua's preferred option. "The captain said—"

"I know what he said."

"You seem like someone who has more important things to do than share your cabin with a roommate you didn't ask for. I'm sure one of those men I met earlier would be up to the task." And more than willing to stay up late discussing bathymetric readings.

Mallory turned, mouth pinched. "I don't trust you around them."

Of course she didn't. Entrancing men was all Mallory had seen her do, so what else could she think? Not enough had changed since the days when church murals portrayed shameless mermaids luring good, innocent, righteous men into their evil nets like hapless, terrified fish. Women who behaved the way Niua behaved were indisputably up to no good.

"If I sleep while my bunkmate is working," Niua explained, even though she was quite sure Mallory didn't need the concept explained to her, "then leave while he sleeps, we won't even see each other."

"Which means no one will be keeping track of you."

Niua winced. "The captain didn't say anyone needed to keep track of me. I'm not a prisoner."

"I'm not convinced the captain made the right call. We don't know why you're here or what you might do, and you won't tell us. Even if you *did* tell us, we wouldn't know whether to believe you. You're an unknown variable."

"You're suspicious. I like that." Suspicious, but not afraid. If Mallory truly thought Niua was dangerous, she wouldn't be putting her in her own cabin.

She wouldn't. Would she?

Mallory shook her head with a barely audible huff of amusement. "You don't give up, do you?"

"Not if it's something worth pursuing."

"I thought I told you your flirting wasn't going to work on me."

"Was that flirting? To say I like you?" Niua refrained from widening her eyes in a show of false innocence. Barely. "I meant it in the spirit of friendship."

"Sure you did."

"I'd like us to be friends." By which she meant, *I'd like you to stop speculating about my motives and ignore me so I can do as I wish.*

"We're stuck with each other in any case." Mallory paused outside a closed door. "To be honest, I don't know whether I'm protecting the guys from you or the other way around."

Again with the caring. Niua didn't quite know what to make of it. "You want to protect me?"

"I shouldn't need to. Everyone's an adult here and the last thing I have time for is to worry about where people are sleeping or who they're…" Mallory shook her head with one sharp movement. "This is not my job."

Someone who worried she might need to be protected. How unexpected. Mallory was misreading the situation, but that was hardly her fault. "I'll be perfectly safe with anyone on this ship."

"Uh-huh."

"I'll be safe, they'll be safe, everyone will behave themselves. There's no need for me to share a bed with you."

"You won't be." Mallory's reply was a bit too quick and a bit too abrupt.

Hmm.

"No?" Niua wanted to smile, but Mallory would think she was flirting and get annoyed. More annoyed.

But the thing was, annoying Mallory was much more entertaining than manipulating helpless, unwitting allies, so she twisted a lock of hair around her finger and allowed the corners of her mouth to twitch upward.

Mallory watched her for one intense moment before pointedly breaking eye contact. "I'm sorry, because it won't be very comfortable, but you'll be sleeping on the floor. Although it will probably be better than wherever you've been sleeping the past few days." She pulled a key from her pocket. "The storage area?"

Niua said nothing, because the only answer she could give would be a lie.

Mallory waited. Finally she gave up and opened the door, securing it in the open position with a click. "Here we are. Home sweet home."

Like every enclosed space on every ship she'd ever set foot on, Mallory's living quarters felt suffocating. There was enough clearance for the door to swing open, and that was about it. A bunk secured to the bulkhead. A tiny desk. The open door to a washroom. There wasn't even a porthole to see whether it was night or day.

A white sheet lay bunched at the foot of the mattress along with a crumpled navy blue duvet. Mallory squeezed around Niua and yanked the covers into some semblance of order.

"Most of the cabins have two bunks, but I was assigned a single because there weren't an even number of women, and the powers that be worry about that sort of thing. And I'm the most senior female." She knelt to pull open a built-in drawer underneath the bed and extracted a neatly folded sheet and blanket. "Do you want my duvet? It's too hot in here for me to want it, but you could sleep on top of it for cushioning."

"The blanket should be more than adequate. Looks comfortable."

"More comfortable than sleeping wedged under spare

equipment?"

"One would imagine so."

"Inside a supply bin?" Mallory pressed.

"Would that be big enough?"

"How should I know?" Mallory shut the drawer, stood up, and stacked the sheet and blanket on her bed. "There aren't many places on this ship where no one would've seen you."

Mallory wasn't going to let this go. It must be the scientist in her, always searching for explanations. Niua would have to watch out for that.

Niua took the bedding, intending to move it to the floor in a corner where it should be out of the way, but she found herself hugging it, unable to keep from fingering the smooth sheet, marveling at the ability to weave material this fine.

In her other form, she didn't need sleep. Like dolphins and other sea creatures who were always in motion, half her brain stayed awake while the other rested. But when she had legs, her physiology changed, and the promise of a clean sheet and a pile of soft bedding made her breath catch. She'd almost forgotten what it was like to sleep in comfort instead of curled between awkwardly shaped rocks or huddled for warmth with ill-tempered seals on one of the ever-harder-to-find uninhabited, undeveloped sections of shoreline where she dared close her eyes for more than an hour at a time. She missed the days when she and the other mermaids would spend their month of nights ashore in human form in small groups, one keeping watch while the others slept. That hadn't happened in a very long time. Mermaids didn't die of natural causes, but they did die. And they had. She was the only one left.

She looked up from the sheet and realized Mallory was staring at her oddly. Niua let the sheet drop and pretended there was nothing remarkable about sleeping on bed linens. Near someone who cared about keeping her safe.

"You're not going to tell me, are you?" Mallory said.

Niua swallowed. *She doesn't know. She thinks you're a spy. An utterly human spy.* "Tell you what?"

"Where you hid."

"Oh." Niua tried not to look relieved. "No."

"I could retrieve your belongings if you tell me where they are. If you need a change of clothes for tomorrow."

"I didn't bring any other clothes."

"You travel light." Mallory looked her up and down as if Niua might be hiding additional layers of clothing under her dress that she'd somehow failed to notice. Her gaze lingered on the bracelet that spiraled around Niua's forearm. Was it suspicious to have jewelry but not extra clothes? Mallory reopened the drawer under the bed and pulled out a pair of black shorts, a gray T-shirt, and an equally gray tank top. She tossed them onto Niua's sheet. "These should fit."

"That's highly optimistic." They'd be tight. And she didn't care for shorts.

"If they're too small, I'll find something else. And I'll track down a pair of coveralls and work boots from one of the guys for you later, see if anyone has extras they're willing to spare."

"Thanks." She should have lied about not having clothes. It was just one more clue Mallory was going to mull over, and it would have been easy enough to borrow from a man herself if wearing the same dress day after day—the same torn dress—started to be noticed as odd.

"If it gets too hot in here, turn on this fan." Mallory touched the switch on the fan secured beside the bed, and an artificial breeze tossed Niua's hair. "Want me to leave it on?"

"Are you leaving me here?" Her heart rate kicked up. "You're not locking me in."

"I'm not locking you in."

Niua edged toward the open door.

Mallory watched her do it, but made no move to stop her. "You can always unlock the door from the inside."

Niua ran her hands over the hardware on both sides of the door and pushed at the latch, testing it. Good. She was telling the truth.

Mallory sighed. "Go ahead and escape if you want to."

"I thought you wanted to keep track of me."

"I changed my mind."

"Because I'm harmless?"

"Because you followed me to my cabin even though you didn't have to." Mallory curled the fingers of one hand into her palm, then extended them one at a time, tapping them to tick off her points. "Because I seem to be the only one who thinks you're capable of stealing anything, and maybe that means I'm wrong. Because even if I'm right, I'm starting to wonder why it matters. Because if you're dead set on jumping, I doubt I could stop you again. Because I have work to do, and I'm tired of worrying about what you're doing here. So…" She made a *what-can-you-do?* motion with her hands. "Stay. Go. I don't care."

Niua stopped fussing with the latch.

"I need to get back to the lab." Mallory angled the fan so it blew toward the floor, toward where Niua would be sleeping.

She obviously wanted her to stay. But why, if not to keep an eye on her?

Mallory moved to the door, and Niua stepped farther inside to make room for her.

"Try not to steal anything while I'm gone. Or break anything. Or sabotage the equipment. Or…you know. Whatever your plan is, that I'm not going to like. It would be nice if you just…didn't." Mallory slid past her and paused outside the doorway. "You should get some rest."

"Right. So I'll be full of energy to swab the deck tomorrow."

"I think the captain may have been joking about that."

"I don't think captains ever joke about free labor."

"I suppose we'll find out," Mallory said. "My shift ends at midnight. I'll be back after then. I'll try to remember you're here and not step on you."

Niua didn't tell her the seals were clumsier and far less polite.

5

When Mallory woke the next morning, wishing she hadn't stayed up quite so late the night before, the door to the washroom was open. Niua was in there with her face in the sink, holding her hair back with one hand, drinking water straight from the tap.

Mallory sat up in bed. "You should've asked me if the water was safe to drink."

"I have a strong stomach," Niua said in between gulps. "Also, I'm assuming you would have phrased that differently if the water wasn't potable."

She was right about that. A fact which Mallory really shouldn't find so aggravating. "You're still here."

Niua shut off the water and raised her head. Her lips were wet. "I thought that's what you wanted."

"I thought what I wanted didn't matter to you."

"It doesn't."

Charming.

Niua let her hair tumble free around her shoulders. "But I've decided our friendship will be more successful if I agree to a few of your requests."

"You mean lull me into a false sense of security."

"Are you like this with all your friends?"

Niua turned the tap back on and splashed water on her face. And the back of her neck. And the front of her neck, tipping her chin up to get as wet as she could, dampening the collar of the gray cotton T-shirt Mallory had loaned her. It possibly—probably—

wasn't flirtatious, but Mallory did not have the mental energy to witness it first thing in the morning.

She collapsed back onto the mattress and hid her face in her pillow. "We're not friends."

"We could be."

Mallory kept her eyes squeezed shut. She hated sharing a cabin. Ships were always packed with too many people in very little space, and she liked her privacy. Deprive her of it for too long and her natural distaste for socializing with coworkers became glaringly obvious. This trip, by some miracle, she'd landed a solo cabin. And then what did she go and do? Even though she knew she'd regret it?

It was fine. She could survive sharing a cabin. She'd survived it before. All sharing meant was sleeping and dressing and storing stuff. It did not have to mean talking, at least not anything beyond a grunt that sounded vaguely like *good morning* and possibly *goodnight* or *do you mind if I turn off the light now?* It did not have to mean breathing the same cabin air while awake.

Niua would figure that out soon enough.

Maybe Mallory could go back to sleep and Niua would give up.

She could use another hour of sleep. It'd been hard to drift off the night before, enclosed in a dark cabin with a stranger she didn't trust. She hadn't honestly believed Niua would murder her while she lay unconscious, but her body hadn't been convinced.

"Mallory."

Mallory grumbled into her pillow.

"Are you getting up?"

"Later."

Niua was undeterred. "If I'm going to be conscripted to work today, I'd prefer it if you could first show me where to get breakfast."

"You expect me to believe you don't have the entire ship's layout memorized?"

"You expect me to believe *you* want me wandering around the ship unsupervised?"

"Yes." If it meant she could sleep another few minutes, then yes.

"Mallory." Niua sounded closer. She sounded like she was looming over her. "Get up."

Mallory should probably shift to a less vulnerable position, but she couldn't find it within herself to worry. And the pillow was cozy.

"Up," Niua said. "Breakfast."

"Go without me."

"Friends accompany each other to meals."

"I told you. We're not friends."

"We should be."

Mallory smiled into the pillow despite herself. She wasn't entertained by this strange creature. She wasn't.

"I know you're awake," Niua said. It felt like she was...was she...touching the bedsheets? Slowly easing them down? Like that was okay?

Mallory reluctantly turned to look.

Yes. Yes, she was.

Niua grinned as if watching Mallory open her eyes, no matter how begrudgingly, was something to be excited about.

Niua winked. "You're going to love being my friend."

Mallory held her breath and visualized herself walking on the sandy seafloor as she led Niua through the ship's passageways to the mess.

They paused at a narrow watertight door and moved aside to allow two scientists coming from the other direction to pass.

Mallory had mastered the art of curt nods and polite smiles and friendly waves, because if she made eye contact she might have to speak, and speaking required opening her mouth, and opening her mouth after long minutes of holding her breath could be awkward, and she didn't enjoy embarrassing herself by gasping for air. The rumor around the university where she worked was that she suffered from some weird asthmatic condition. She'd never bothered to set the record straight, although it irritated her to be the subject of gossip, and irritated her even more that people weren't careful not to be overheard, no matter how much she told herself she didn't care what they thought of her.

She could just breathe normally, of course. She could train her lungs for freediving in private. She didn't have to multitask.

Nah. She'd rather avoid the polite small talk.

One of the men nodded in greeting as he passed; the other one rubbed his forehead like he had a headache and ignored them. Mallory smiled. They were the kind of colleagues she got along with: silent ones.

The ship swayed, and that was the end of it. She exhaled as she caught her balance, then inhaled as subtly as possible and checked her dive watch to note how many seconds she'd lasted.

Niua didn't seem to notice. She stepped around Mallory and reached her arms wide to grip the metal sides of the doorway. She looked like a kid playing dress-up in the too-large coveralls and sturdy work boots Mallory had borrowed for her late last night from one of the crewmembers.

"You steady?" Mallory asked, waiting for her to step through. There was a raised doorsill which prevented water from sloshing from one section of the ship to another, and the only reason she could think of why Niua didn't just step over it was she was having trouble keeping her balance.

"Of course." Niua stuck her head through the opening, her feet glued in place, and leaned confidently forward as if she were a fish gliding through the skeleton of a sunken ship.

Mallory wasn't sure what happened next. The ship's motion wasn't bad, yet somehow Niua fell, catching both her shins on the sill and landing on her knees, her forearms, and possibly her face.

"Aargh!" Niua curled into a fetal position, hiding her head in her arms and wheezing shallowly.

"Are you all right?"

A quiet *ow* was her only response.

Mallory knelt at her side. Were Niua's boots so heavy she hadn't lifted her feet high enough to clear the sill? Because no one would forget to lift their feet—not when they couldn't possibly have not seen the obstacle. Even if Mallory had a feeling that was exactly what happened.

She touched Niua's shoulder in concern, then let go uncertainly. Was she injured and needed help? Was she embarrassed and wanted to be left alone? Did she want to be fussed over and comforted? Mallory wasn't good at fussing. Hugs she could do, but when a woman expected words, Mallory's attempts, she'd been told, were lacking. "Are you hurt?"

"I'll live." Niua wriggled away, humping along the floor like a seal.

Rejection. Of course. Mallory should give her space. "Want me to go find the medical officer?"

"No need." Niua scrambled to her feet as if nothing had happened. Her face was red but not obviously bruised. "Just a stumble."

Apparently she didn't want to be comforted.

Which was good.

Wonderful.

Really.

Mallory frowned. "You fell really hard."

"Looked worse than it was."

Mallory hadn't imagined the sight of her curled in pain, but she let it go.

Mallory motioned for Niua to go through the buffet queue without her while Mallory got coffee, which was at a separate station. "Take a tray and help yourself."

"What dish do you recommend?"

Mallory shrugged. "It's all edible."

"Okay." Niua looked a bit lost, but got in the queue.

What had she been doing for food for the past several days, anyway? Mallory had assumed she'd been stealing food from the twenty-four-hour buffet, but she must have had a stash in her hiding place. Now that everyone was watching her, she wouldn't want to go near it and risk her supplies being discovered. Her incriminating supplies. Which would include the clothes she pretended not to have. Because she *must* have boarded with spare clothes.

Mallory turned around to check on her. Niua had an empty plate and no one was queued up behind her.

That was odd. It wasn't as if there weren't people coming in. There were.

But then, as Mallory watched, one man after another grabbed a tray, headed for the buffet, spotted Niua, hesitated, and decided he wasn't hungry.

Yeah, they had reason to be embarrassed. They'd acted like lovestruck idiots the day before. She didn't understand why this morning they weren't drooling over her or ogling her or trying to get her attention, but, whatever the reason, it was a relief. Mallory was here to work, not to watch her shipmates go into heat. Or to puzzle over why, eighteen hours later, they suddenly weren't.

Coffee in hand, Mallory rejoined Niua in the buffet queue, and Hudson, the geophysicist who'd allowed a barefoot stranger to look over his shoulder at their data instead of immediately escorting her to the captain like he should have, joined in behind her. She should talk with him later. He might be able to shed some light on what Niua had been after in the lab.

"Hope I didn't come on too strong yesterday," Hudson told Niua, speaking to her over Mallory's head. "I know we talked, but my memory of our conversation is weirdly hazy."

"You were a perfect gentleman," Niua said.

She seemed to be having trouble handling the tongs for the bacon. Hudson reached over to help, leaning across Mallory as if she weren't there. Because apparently she was invisible.

"I don't know what happened," Hudson said. "My head is killing me. Tell me I don't have a concussion."

Niua looked surprisingly unsympathetic. "Did you fall?"

"Don't think so. Would I remember, though? If I did?"

"I'm sure it's simply the effect of a poor night's sleep," Niua said.

"Or a brain tumor." Hudson landed two strips of bacon onto Niua's plate.

"A sudden-onset brain tumor? Is that likely?"

"It's not impossible. You don't happen to have any aspirin on you, do you?"

"No. Sorry."

"Mallory?" Hudson turned to her with a hopeful pout.

Mallory didn't have the patience to make the effort to not look annoyed, so she reached into the buffet for a roasted tomato so she'd have an excuse not to look at him. "Try the medical officer."

"Morning," chimed in Santos, another one of the geophysicists, as he joined the queue. He was one of the guys who'd shied away from Niua a minute ago, but apparently he was willing to approach now that he could do so without having to stand too close to her. "Got any painkillers?"

"You, too?" Mallory said.

"Does that mean no?" Santos said.

"Who has paracetamol? Hit me up," bellowed someone else from the door.

Santos clapped his hands over his ears and jerked away from the noise, somehow managing to knock Mallory's coffee cup from her tray. Mallory jumped out of the way just in time to avoid getting splashed, but the floor needed help.

"Sorry," Santos said, making no move to do anything about it.

Mallory snatched the cup off the floor before it could roll away. "What, did everyone get hammered last night?"

"Like I need another reason to throw up," Hudson said.

"Vomit Boy gets seasick," Santos said.

"Shut up," Hudson said.

"Some of us can handle a little excitement," Santos shot back.

"So it is alcohol?" Mallory said. Weren't they capable of drinking without ending up like this the next morning?

"Sadly, no." Santos closed his eyes.

"Then what happened to you?" Mallory said. It couldn't be

seasickness—she'd be the first to feel queasy if the sea was acting up.

"Don't know," Santos grumbled.

"You never do," Hudson said.

"Shut up," Santos said. "All of you. It's too loud in here."

Ah, the joys of being trapped on a boat with other people. If she survived the next week and a half of this, she was going to lock herself in her lab and refuse to see anyone for at least a month. Or a year—she hadn't decided yet.

She gave up on the buffet and walked to the tub of dirty dishes to dispose of her cup, poured herself a fresh cup, and confessed to June, the crewperson who was replacing the hot water urn, that she'd made a mess.

"I'll take care of it," June said. "Still getting your sea legs?"

"It wasn't my fault this time," Mallory grumbled.

June had warned her when she came aboard that she hadn't forgotten how they'd met. It'd been several years ago during Mallory's first time aboard the *Sea Monster*. The weather was bad, the waves high, and Mallory had accidentally doused June with hot coffee. June had shrugged it off, and they'd developed an easy camaraderie. She was one of the few crewmembers from that expedition who hadn't since been replaced by new faces.

"I told the captain we should give all the scientists sippy cups with lids," June said.

"I'll take one right now if you have one."

"He said he'd consider it. Said you were all babies."

Mallory grimaced. June seemed to appreciate his brand of humor more than Mallory did. "Sounds like something he would say."

June set the urn into position. "Heard you got yourself a roommate."

"News travels fast."

"Nothing else to do around here but work and gossip." June grinned as she leaned in and lowered her voice. "So. Is this mystery woman as hot as everyone's saying?"

"She's in the buffet queue, in front of the toast. Decide for yourself."

June looked over and stared a little longer than was polite. "Huh. She's pretty, I suppose."

Pretty? She wasn't *pretty*. She was different. Compelling. Not traditionally stunning, but... well... it was easy to find herself watching her, even when she didn't want to. Mallory scowled. She had more important things to do than wonder whether Niua was attractive. Many, many things. Tons.

"Not quite what I was expecting from the way the guys were talking." June looked again, as if maybe she'd missed something the first time. "I mean, you heard them, didn't you?"

"I try not to listen when they talk about women."

"You like to keep things professional," June said understandingly.

"I get that it's hard to do when we're together twenty-four/seven, but yes."

"You're so annoying. Go eat before I convince you that gossiping is way more fun."

"June. I didn't mean—"

June smiled and shooed her away. "I know. It's fine. Go."

Mallory hesitated, but June was leaving with the empty urn, so she took her at her word and left.

When she reached the table Niua and Hudson had commandeered, the two of them were already eating. Hudson was still discussing his headache.

"I don't know what happened," he insisted. "My memory's all hazy."

A flash of amusement crossed Niua's face. What was *that* about? Mallory would have thought she'd be cooing at him with compassion, not whatever this was, smiling like she knew a secret he didn't. But far be it from her to assume a woman was a psychopath if *my poor baby* wasn't her heartfelt response to everyone else's pain.

"Mind if I join you?" Mallory asked.

Hudson gestured to the seat beside him. "Sit."

Niua now seemed to be completely engrossed in fishing a single dry bran flake from her cereal bowl with her fingers.

"What about ibuprofen?" Hudson asked. "Have any of that, Mallory?"

"Still no."

"Hard drugs? Nothing?"

Maybe there really was something going on with his head. She hesitated, clutching her tray, uncertain whether she should sit. Surely the last thing he wanted was to endure the company of someone he barely knew. "Are you all right?"

"I've been better," Hudson said.

Niua held the bran flake to her lips and nibbled at it with all the caution and concentration of someone conducting an important taste test.

Mallory realized she was staring at Niua's mouth.

She still hadn't taken a seat.

Niua paused between nibbles, swallowed, and tilted her head quizzically in Mallory's direction.

And smiled.

Mallory hadn't seen her smile face-on before, and it was only now that she noticed there was a gap on the upper left side where a tooth was missing. Niua didn't keep her lips pressed together to hide her missing tooth like it was something to be ashamed of, like she cared what anyone else thought she was supposed to look like.

Her defiance was dazzling. It made her beautiful. That imperfect smile was the sexiest thing Mallory had seen in a long time.

If she found her sexy.

Which she didn't.

She really should sit. If she didn't stop hovering, this was going to become awkward. Maybe at a different table, though, if she could do it without making it look like a snub. Niua wasn't alone and abandoned and hoping for company. She had Hudson right there with her. They didn't need anyone else.

She was overthinking this. She set her tray down next to Niua's.

Even though the ship was barely swaying, her coffee sloshed over the edge of her cup and spilled onto the tray.

"Can I get you a spoon?" she asked Niua.

"Oh. I..." Niua glanced at her cereal in surprise, like she was only just now noticing she had no silverware.

Hudson thrust his spoon at her from across the table. "Have mine. I haven't touched it."

"Thank you." Niua fluttered her eyelashes at him. Mallory couldn't help but notice that her smile was gone, replaced by an irritatingly winsome pout that probably got men to do her all sorts of favors.

"Can I get you a spoon?" Mallory asked Hudson in exasperation, since he, too, had a bowl of cereal in front of him.

"Why?" he said, glancing up in confusion, then at his bowl. "Oh. No. I'll get it." He rubbed his forehead and rose from the table.

"How long do you think it takes for one of these to dissolve?" Niua said, and spooned a single bran flake into her mouth. She sucked on the spoon and wrapped her lips tightly around it as she slowly pulled it free.

Mallory sighed. How many more days of this?

Well, she didn't have to watch. Next time she was sitting at a different table.

Alone.

6

When Niua reported to the trawl deck after breakfast, it turned out she was not there to swab the deck, but to police it.

According to Courtland, who was to be her supervisor—and who had not said a word about fishing her out of the sea, since the memory had doubtlessly been safely muddled by his subsequent headache—the scientists tended to get overly excited about the rock samples dredged from the seafloor and make a nuisance of themselves when the crew was operating the winch.

"Boys and girls," Courtland said to the group assembled in a cordoned-off area of the open deck. "If you haven't already met her, this is Niua. She is the adult in charge. May I remind you that the rope has been placed here for your safety. You will stay behind the rope until she informs you it is safe to proceed."

One of the scientists—an older man with a thinning gray ponytail—let out a pained sigh. "Safety," he muttered.

Niua crossed her arms and tried to look intimidating. It wasn't her usual approach to getting what she wanted, but if she cast her spell on them, they'd be following her around like infatuated pilot fish until the effect wore off, and she'd had enough of that for the time being. She could do this the human way. The non-magical way.

Besides, they weren't all men. There were two women she hadn't seen before chatting at the very front of the group, and of course there was Mallory, who had squeezed in at the back of the group and was jockeying for position while holding a plastic bucket in front of her like a shield.

The scientists fidgeted.

Perhaps frowning would help.

She glanced down at herself and noticed her arms were pushing her breasts up.

Perhaps not sticking out her chest would help.

She uncrossed her arms and straightened her spine. Aargh. Straight—not arching. She adjusted her posture again. She could do this.

The coveralls Mallory had found for her covered her from neck to wrist to ankle in baggy, ill-fitting, waterproof, high-visibility orange glory. Add the standard work boots and a hardhat, and no doubt Mallory imagined this would stop the men from noticing her. Niua snorted. Poor Mallory had no idea what Niua could do to this crew if she chose. And she didn't have to show skin to do it.

With the scientists corralled, the dredge was lowered into the sea. It would make contact with the seafloor and be dragged along by the forward motion of the ship to scoop up whatever it encountered. Ooze, she supposed, along with loose rocks and slime. It didn't sound all that interesting to her.

She tugged down the zipper at her neck and unstuck the clammy material from her sweaty chest. When she let go, it stuck again. Intolerable. Amazing that a civilization capable of weaving such soft sheets would willingly wear such clothing—especially in the relentless heat.

She slid the zipper back up a few notches, trying to find the perfect position to allow maximum airflow but not reveal cleavage. She'd save that for later—when she wanted to annoy Mallory. For now, it would be better for Mallory to focus on the work that seemed so important to her and lose the wrinkle between her eyes. And better for Niua to stop feeling the urge to smooth that wrinkle away.

"Niua!" It was Courtland. "Heads up!"

Niua glanced over with a start. The dredge was emerging from the sea, swinging on its cable as it rose above them, seawater dripping from the bag of steel chain mesh attached to a scoop.

She backed out of the way and stationed herself in front of a knot of scientists who watched the dredge with the intensity of gannets hovering in the sky, preparing for the perfect moment to dive straight down into the ocean and snatch a fish. There was no guardrail at that end. The dredge was big, and it was full of heavy, jagged rocks, and it was swinging awkwardly toward the deck. Did these highly educated people really need her to remind them to steer clear?

Courtland moved forward to help as Giancarlo and Omar, the other winch operators, caught it, guided the mesh bag into position above the designated dumping spot, and let its contents tumble out.

The rocks hit the deck hard and rolled. Giancarlo guided the dredge out of the way as scientists scrambled over Niua's flimsy rope and out of her illusory holding pen. They dived in, eagerly stripping seaweed off the pile and tossing it aside to be hosed off the deck later, then carefully placing unremarkable rocks in buckets like they were pirate treasure.

Courtland weaved his way through, plucking out plastic water bottles, a toothbrush, torn fishing nets, and other debris. He tossed one of the pieces to Niua.

"What is it?" she asked as she caught it. She wasn't sure what she was expected to do with this…object. The slimy plastic cube was the size of her hand. Was she on cleanup duty now, or was this valuable?

"You've never seen a Rubik's Cube?" Courtland untangled a length of damaged netting from the rocks. "What planet are you from?"

Oh dear. She should have held her tongue. Her vaguely foreign accent, no matter what language she spoke, was usually enough to excuse any gaps in her cultural knowledge. But not this time.

Courtland shook his head. "You must be too young."

Ah, good. He could rationalize her gaffe.

"Back in the eighties, these puppies were the hottest toy in the universe."

"A square ball?" She tossed it in the air and caught it.

Courtland snorted a laugh and motioned for the cube, so she tossed it back to him. He tried to twist it, but nothing happened. "Stuck. No surprise. Sand got inside and cemented everything together." He wrestled with it again. Still nothing. "You've really never seen one? All the brainy kids had one. Even if you weren't one of the—"

"I'll take that." Mallory rose from the rock huddle, hand extended like the cube belonged to her, glaring at Courtland like she dared him to say anything further about Niua's intellect.

"It's useless," Courtland said. "Won't move."

"It's scientific evidence," Mallory countered.

"Evidence of what?" Courtland muttered, handing it over. "Human habitation of every last place on earth?"

"Thank you." Mallory pocketed the cube and returned to the pile of marine detritus.

Niua felt like a wave had come out of nowhere and tumbled her upside down. Had Mallory...defended her?

Squatting, Mallory fished a miniature magnifying glass out of her pocket and held the lens to her eye to give one of the smaller rocks a quick look. Head bowed, she drew the rock closer.

One of the other scientists moved from his spot and stepped over Mallory like she was a rock herself. He was far too close, and Mallory lost her balance. She fell to her knees on the rocks, dropping the piece she'd been holding but saving her hand lens.

"Watch it!" the man beside her barked, yanking his bucket out of her path and setting it farther away. "Don't damage the rocks."

Like the dredge hadn't been rougher.

"The rocks can handle it." She placed the rock in her bucket and selected another one to examine.

The man who'd complained moved to another spot.

To all appearances, Mallory was so focused on her work that nothing else around her existed. But she'd been listening. She'd been paying attention. She'd taken the cube from Courtland.

She hadn't said a word to Niua, though.

Which was good. Excellent. The less anyone noticed her, the more invisible she became, the more easily she'd sneak into the area that housed that bank of computers and find a way to access the sonar data.

Niua was happy to be ignored.

Thrilled.

Really.

That compulsion to wait for Mallory to make eye contact? Unhelpful. Mallory already made her feel seen—and that was dangerously close to being known.

This woman was a deep-sea current that could pull her off course.

Niua couldn't allow that to happen.

She could ignore the pull—*would* ignore the pull—no matter how attractive Mallory was. No matter how focused, intent, passionate, and single-minded she was. No matter how much it hurt to hear her silence herself in order to get along with colleagues who acted like she was in their way.

Niua's sole priority was to convince Mallory her stowaway fit in as part of the crew and no longer needed to be kept away from sensitive data. And then she'd get what she came for and bid this ship farewell.

That evening, as soon as Niua was released from her duties on deck—the scientists and crew all worked twelve-hour shifts, but Courtland didn't hold her to it—she found her way to the geophysics lab.

Hudson sat in the same seat she'd found him in the day before. He was happy to show her the data they'd collected that showed the shape of the seafloor, but there wasn't much. They'd been at sea for less than a week, it seemed, and there were no earlier records to refer to, as this expedition was the first to map this particular area of the Indian Ocean in detail.

"People don't realize how little we know about the ocean," Hudson said, eager to launch into lecture mode. He clicked enthusiastically through the images displayed on the array of monitors. "There could be mountains down there as high as the Himalayas. And we'd have no idea."

"Mountains? My goodness." Niua tried hard not to sound like a mother indulging a small child as he rambled on about his amazing discoveries on the playground. The resolution of the images was good enough that a shipwreck should be evident—if they passed directly over it.

"Mountains, volcanoes, canyons, trenches… No one has a clue what's down there. Not in any detail. We know less about the bottom of the sea than we do about the surface of the moon." His fingers jittered on the keyboard, causing another set of images to appear. "This is cutting-edge science."

"Hmm." Should she tell him that was fascinating? Or would that be too much? She cocked her head at the inadequate charts around her, the pinnacle of human exploration. She opened her mouth, but she couldn't do it. Which was all right. She didn't need to fawn over him. Just…express some interest. "How long will the ship stay in this area?"

"Only eight more days. If it weren't for the marine mammal regulations, we could be running the air guns more consistently and acquiring more data."

More data? Niua perked up. "What regulations?"

"Oh, you know. Can't start up the air guns if a whale gets too close."

"Really?"

Hudson nodded. "Daphne—she's the MMO—that's the marine mammal observer—has to watch for at least an hour and give the all-clear before we can get started. Kind of makes me want to invent a whale communication device so we could just tell them to get the heck out, you know?" He cupped his hands around his mouth in the shape of a bullhorn and spoke in a garbled, tinny voice. "Can I have your attention, please. Attention all cetaceans and pinnipeds. This is a safety announcement. Please identify yourselves to authorized personnel and leave the area immediately. I repeat, this is a safety announcement."

"You wait until they're gone?"

"That's correct."

"But you don't in fact know whether they're near unless you see them surface."

"They want to stay below for an hour, they're on their own. We can't wait all day."

Niua blinked. She'd had no idea these scientists understood their deafening explosions were hazardous. Or that they cared. About whales, at least. Clearly not about all sea life. Fish, for example, were out of luck. They could be scared away from their habitat and this MMO observer person would never know. Crabs? Clams? Sea urchins? They were too slow to escape, and clearly not worth worrying about.

"So you lose an hour each day." On a well-meaning gesture of limited scope.

"More than that, because the ramp-up takes a while. That's to warn the stragglers. Fire one air gun... wait... add another one... wait... add another one... wait..." He ran his fingers over his scalp and grabbed what he could of his close-cropped hair. "Wait..." He pulled. "Wait..."

"You could listen for the whales underwater," she said. They didn't sing all the time, but...

"Some people do that, yeah. But it doesn't work. It's noisy down there, you know."

No kidding.

"The software that's supposed to identify whale songs? Pick them out from all the other sounds?" He contorted his lower lip like he'd tasted something bad. "Not reliable."

Was there a way she could speed up the process without exposing herself? Teach them how to hear the whales underwater instead of waiting for the creatures to surface? She doubted it. But she wasn't ruling it out.

7

Their charts were useless. Yes, the ship was scanning Niua's target area, but that area was unfortunately quite large. Hudson and the others could certainly survey more of the ocean floor more quickly than Niua could on her own, swimming search patterns, but she couldn't afford to stay and wait for them to collect new data.

The moon was beginning to wane. She needed to think about leaving.

She wasn't sure how many years it had taken her to swim from her current haunts off the Shetland Islands to the other side of the world, floating in currents and hitching rides in swirling gyres which sped her down the coast of Africa, around the cape, and onward, drifting like flotsam in the company of sea turtles conserving their energy, lost athletic shoes, and plastic detritus bleached bone white by the sun.

A decade? At least that.

Since the day she'd learned what happened to the chalice.

She'd been loitering one night outside a houseboat docked in its slip, hiding in the shadows cast by the lights of the sleepy marina, bobbing in the water and watching television through the boat's window. An ornately framed painting of a cutlass-wielding pirate on the deck of a ship with a damsel clinging to his shoulders flashed across the screen.

"Lennart the Pirate is the stuff of legend," the voice-over explained. "In his most brazen—and final—heist, he escaped with dozens of priceless artifacts from France's Atlantic Museum of Art and Antiquities and sailed away from the Port of Dunkirk, never to be heard from again. Whether the curator's daughter was a willing accomplice who joined him in his getaway or whether he kidnapped her is unknown." A sketch replaced the painting on the screen. "Among the items stolen was this gold cup, unearthed three hundred years ago during the excavation of a churchyard in Brittany."

The chalice. *Her* chalice.

Niua stopped breathing.

"The artifact was believed by researchers of the time to be a religious relic associated with the church, which saved it from being melted down for its gold."

A Christian relic? What? Her fists clenched, aching to hold her long-lost treasure.

"But modern archaeologists believe it to be much older than the church itself, likely Bronze Age."

Her body tingled with the memory of its song.

"This sketch is the sole record that remains of any of the treasures stolen from the museum. But now, according to Dr. Adam Hollingshead, a researcher at the Museum of Indo-Pacific Marine Archaeology and Maritime Anthropology in Perth, Australia, who was contacted out of the blue by an intrigued homeowner, a one-hundred-eighty-seven-year-old diary has been discovered behind the walls of a home under renovation on a remote, sparsely inhabited island in the Indian Ocean that provides an eyewitness account of the pirate ship's sinking during a violent storm."

Niua could barely stay afloat. She'd forgotten how to move, afraid to miss a word, even if each revelation was a punch to the gut. The chalice had been within reach—in a poorly guarded museum—and she'd never known. And now it was gone again.

The chalice had returned to the sea.

She'd saved it, once, by diving with it in her arms into the ocean's embrace.

She'd fled south with the other mermaids until the coastline of familiar deltas and sand dunes gave way to rocky cliffs, until they'd found a sea cave to hide it in.

Where, eventually, it was stolen.

It didn't belong in a shipwreck or a museum or a church or even a cave.

It belonged with her tribe. But her tribe was gone. Now the chalice belonged with her, connecting past and future, a tool only she and the goddess understood.

If biding her time here on the *Sea Monster*, scanning the waters near the archipelago where the pirate ship had last been seen, wasn't going to help her find the ship and rescue the chalice, then the best thing to do with the precious time she had remaining would be to narrow her search area by going ashore and tracking down the exact place where the diary had been found.

But on which of these islands had the diarist lived? In which direction had his home faced? How far could he have seen through his spy glass?

The smooth, authoritative voice hadn't said. Which didn't mean the islanders didn't know. It didn't mean they wouldn't tell her.

She should leave and find out.

Shipwrecks didn't sit, perfectly preserved, on the ocean floor forever. They disintegrated. If she hoped to find the wreck before it disappeared into the sand—or was found by someone else—she had a limited amount of time to do so.

Relationships, too, were ephemeral. The hope of getting to know Mallory had been an unachievable fantasy from the start. She'd planned to stay only another day or two, and that would hardly have been enough.

She twisted a lock of hair around her finger, around and around and around, soothed by the dry rasp against her skin as her hair continuously slipped free. She had only one month.

If I leave now, I'll never see her again.

Yes, well, if she left in two days—or three, or four—she'd get to know her a little more and *then* she'd never see her again. Was that really any better?

Yes, her heart whispered.

Ridiculous heart.

It always won these arguments.

Niua found Mallory in one of the labs. Plastic tubs crammed with rocks crowded every available surface on the long tables that filled the space. Mallory stood working at the only clear spot. The Rubik's Cube lay in pieces spread out on a table. She was scraping and cleaning and lubricating each piece.

Mallory didn't seem to have heard Niua's footfall as she approached the open doorway, nor her breathing when she came to a stop and wordlessly leaned against the doorframe, waiting for Mallory to notice her.

Of course not. The hum of the ship's engine was too loud, and Mallory was focused on her task.

Niua fingered the metal zipper pull at the neck of the coveralls she'd been wearing since morning. How would it feel to have that intensity focused on her? Solely on her, and nothing else? How breathtaking would it be if, in the depths of Mallory's scrutiny, Niua saw not only sharp intelligence, but also a spark of desire?

She was unlikely to find out.

She shifted uncomfortably on her feet and gripped the edge of the doorway to maintain her balance. She didn't need to find out how it would affect her if Mallory looked at her—and touched her—like she mattered. She'd had a hint of it when Mallory had dressed her in a man's too-large shirt, and if that was all she ever got, it would have to be enough. She rarely allowed herself to indulge in regrets, and she wasn't going to start now.

Time passed, and at last Mallory assembled all the pieces and affixed brightly colored stickers—the ones they used to label their sampling containers—so each side of the cube was a single color.

Another scientist approached in the passageway and paused at the door. Niua slithered out of his way and pretended she wasn't standing there idle, looking suspicious.

He walked past without acknowledging her and entered the lab. "You done in here, Mallory? This is my time slot."

Mallory fumbled the cube in surprise and dropped it into the nearest tub of rocks. "I'll be out of your hair in a minute."

When Niua returned to their cabin sometime after midnight, she found Mallory sitting in bed in a stretchy tank top and holding the Rubik's Cube, the sheet bunched in her lap.

"According to Courtland, that object means you were one of the intelligent children," Niua said, stripping off her uncomfortable coveralls and changing into the clothes meant for sleeping which Mallory had loaned her. She'd prefer a nightdress over the tank and shorts Mallory had deemed appropriate, but she supposed she could tolerate the sensation of fabric encasing her thighs, a nagging reminder she'd have to strip when it came time to escape. How strange that she could forget how it felt to have two lower limbs, when it had once been the most natural thing in the world.

Mallory kept her gaze fixed determinedly on her own lap. "I think it has more to do with pattern recognition than true intelligence."

Niua spread out her blanket in the cramped space on the floor. "Mm?"

"I didn't have a lot of friends when I was a kid, so I'd spend hours mastering this thing."

"You're saying it was brute persistence?"

"That was certainly part of it. It was good preparation for doing lab work, actually. In the lab, you have to be able to put up with long stretches of boredom and believe the exciting parts will make it worth it." She looked over and seemed relieved to find Niua dressed. "I shouldn't have wasted time cleaning this. I should've been cleaning rock samples. But..."

"You're allowed to do something fun once in a while." Niua shook out her bedsheet and laid it on the blanket. "What is the goal?"

Mallory's smile turned radiant, like Niua had said something that pleased her. She offered her the cube. "Why don't you give it a shot?"

She patted the bed in invitation, and Niua climbed on beside her, kneeling and settling on one hip.

She took the cube. "What do I do with it?"

Mallory covered Niua's hands with her own, and together they rotated one section. The cube creaked. The colors shifted.

"See?" Mallory sounded more excited than was warranted.

All Niua saw was their hands, Mallory's skin pale against her own. Niua tightened her grip on the cube, and the edges—straighter and flatter than anything found in nature—dug into her palms. It made her even more aware of Mallory's gentle hold.

Don't let go. Stay.

Mallory released her.

Niua sat there stupidly staring at the cube without seeing it. She could still feel the remembered pressure of Mallory's fingers.

"Turn it," Mallory encouraged.

Niua turned one side, the side Mallory had rotated, returning it to its starting position, aligning the squares so each side was all one color.

"It doesn't turn as smoothly as I'd hoped," Mallory said, sounding apologetic.

Niua had no idea how it compared to its original, pre-submerged state, but in her opinion, it moved reasonably well. She rotated the side again. Then the top. Then another side, scrambling the colors. The changing patterns were nice. She turned it again, lining up three squares. "It's the act of creating order out of chaos." She tried to add a fourth square, and the three split apart. "But chaos always wins."

"Not when I do it." Niua hadn't expected Mallory to sound so...resigned? "I loved that thing when I was learning it, but now...I don't know. I know I can solve it. So there's no point."

"You find joy in discovery."

Mallory gave her a sharp look that showed Niua how it would

feel to be one of those rocks of hers. "That's exactly it."

Niua's skin warmed. She liked knowing she was the reason for the excited spark in Mallory's eyes.

"The puzzle has a clear goal," Mallory explained, "and once you understand how the pieces move, that goal can always be reached. Always. I never wonder how it will turn out. I *know* how it'll turn out. Even if I encounter a color combination I've never seen before, I know exactly what to do. That's…"

"Boring?"

"Yeah. It feels like a waste of time. There's no mystery."

And here Niua was, a living puzzle who was nothing if not a mystery. Mallory's words were a reminder to stay on her guard. Niua wasn't feeling nearly as nervous as she ought to.

"Why did you repair the cube, then? You could have been examining your rocks."

"Nostalgia, I guess."

Niua lined up a row of pieces along one edge, the colors correctly matched on both sides. But the rest was hopeless. She held it out to Mallory. "Show me?"

Mallory took the cube from her, examined all the sides, then spun the blocks, the colors gravitating toward each other and splitting apart and rejoining. She paused for a barely discernible moment to contemplate her next move, and then her elegant wrists twisted the cube again until all the colors were in their proper places. Faster than should have been possible.

Niua stared. The cube was done. Solved. Perfect.

It was a silly skill to be impressed by, but there it was.

It ought to inspire her to want to master this strangely wonderful object herself. To learn something new.

Not to watch this woman.

To have her.

Niua bit down hard on her bottom lip. "Do it again?"

Mallory swiftly scrambled the cube. She hesitated, reluctantly observing each side but making no attempt to solve it. She tried to pass the cube back to Niua. "Your turn."

Niua sat on her hands and shook her head. "You."

Mallory gave her an assessing look, like she was trying to decide if Niua was making fun of her or pitying her for being interested in something no one else cared about because it was incomprehensible that Niua could have any other reaction. "I feel like a performing seal."

"You don't have to be embarrassed about being good at something."

"I have not found that to be true," Mallory said, but her hands were already moving, the colors lining up as the rows clicked into place.

She handed back the completed cube. This time Niua took it.

"You keep it," Mallory said. "You've already figured out that you need to think of positioning three-dimensional pieces, not single sides. I don't know why, but not everyone gets that."

"Are you complimenting my intelligence, sweetheart?" Niua teased, wishing she'd kept the coveralls on so she could fluster Mallory by sliding her zipper to the edge of her culture's standards of decency. Anything to distract herself from the surprising intensity of this attraction.

Mallory shook her head in exasperation as if she knew what Niua was thinking. "You shouldn't call me that."

Was that a hint of fondness she detected mixed in with the exasperation? Niua was almost certain it was.

Huh.

8

Mallory couldn't sleep. She was too busy hanging on to the grab bar screwed to the bulkhead beside her bed while the ship tossed violently in the rough sea. It would be a miracle if she made it through the night without vomiting.

The ship rolled. There was the sound of something sliding across the floor which could only be Niua. She winced. Could Niua really be sleeping through this?

The ship rolled the other way. Niua slid again.

Mallory shouldn't have made her sleep on the floor. What had she been thinking? She hadn't been thinking, that's what. She still didn't trust her—and how could she, when Niua refused to say why she was on the ship or how she'd stayed hidden for days—but this wasn't fair.

The ship heaved. There was a jarring thump. Niua cried out.

Mallory jerked up, keeping firm hold of the grab bar. "You okay?"

"Go back to sleep," Niua said.

"Niua." That impact had sounded serious.

The ship plunged, and Niua was thrown again. Hit the bulkhead again. Or the furniture. Either one would be painful and dangerous.

A sad whimper came from Niua's direction.

"I'm going to turn on the light," Mallory warned. She'd blind them both, but she needed to know if Niua was hurt. "Close your eyes."

The light revealed Niua curled in a fetal position near the door.

Mallory felt sick—and not because she was seasick. What did it really matter why she'd stowed away on their ship? She didn't deserve this.

"Get in my bunk. If we wedge in together we'll roll around less."

Niua didn't move.

Mallory thought back on what she'd said and cringed. "If you want to. If it doesn't make you uncomfortable."

Niua said nothing.

"Or not. I'll find someplace else for you to sleep. I'll—"

"I want to." Niua flopped onto her other side and another pained cry came out.

"You're hurt." This was the second time in less than twenty-four hours. She seemed to have fully recovered from her fall on the way to breakfast, but that could either be because the incident hadn't been too serious or because Mallory hadn't been paying close enough attention or because Niua was good at hiding her injuries.

"No. I'll...I...need a minute."

That was not good. If she'd been working all day, pretending she wasn't in pain, her new bruises were going to feel even worse. "Want help?"

Niua groaned and pushed herself to her knees. "I'll manage." She crawled to Mallory's bed and clambered in, collapsing on top of the sheet.

An hour later, Niua had snuggled up to Mallory's side, curled an arm around Mallory's ribcage, tucked her head into Mallory's armpit, and fallen asleep.

It was too warm in the stuffy cabin to be touching, even in nothing but tank tops, but Niua's body heat wasn't oppressive. Her breathing was slow and steady and peaceful, and it pulled Mallory in, deepening her own breath as they synchronized with each other. The rolling of the ship moved to the background of her awareness, more a lullaby than an alarm, far less important than the feeling of having Niua in her arms, solid and trusting. At some point she might even be able to sleep.

She stroked Niua's hair softly, careful not to disturb her.

Why had Niua climbed that guardrail?

Not really a question, was it? She knew what she'd been doing. She'd been trying to jump.

Mallory squeezed her protectively. What could have scared Niua so much about being discovered that she'd react like that? She'd struggled violently in Mallory's arms, desperate to free herself, one slip away from tragedy. And now here she was in her arms again, this time voluntarily.

Why had she changed her mind?

If Mallory knew the answer to that, there was a chance she could make sure Niua never tried that again.

But she didn't. She didn't know anything about her at all. Not who she worked for, not why she was aboard the *Sea Monster*, not where she came from.

Was she lonely? In trouble? A danger to the ship? A danger to herself? Why would she turn to a stranger in her sleep and cling to her as trustingly as she would a lover?

Earlier she'd called her *sweetheart*.

No doubt she called everyone *sweetheart* and didn't mean anything by it. It meant nothing.

It hadn't quite felt like nothing.

Mallory had melted a little. She'd wanted it to mean something. Her heart had lurched in pleasure, and she hadn't recovered yet.

She adjusted the way she lay, searching for any way they could possibly be in closer contact. The comfortable weight of Niua's body and her briny scent and her steady breathing overwhelmed Mallory's senses until they were all she could feel.

Diving had taught her to pay attention to her breathing, and although she'd never admit out loud to anything so unscientific, she sometimes imagined that her life was measured not by the steady change in a digital clock readout, standardized and calibrated so each tick lasted precisely as long as the next, but by her own breath. Rushed or slow, conscious or unconscious, purposeful or routine, each inhale carried her through time, counting down the moments until she had no more.

When she held her breath, the countdown was suspended, and she stepped out of her own timeline. And there, unanchored, floating outside of time, she was free. Free to change direction, to choose another path, to allow herself to see things differently.

She felt like that now, contemplating this woman who'd crawled into bed with her without hesitation. What would it be like to kiss her? To let her scent and her mouth and her fearlessness overwhelm her even more?

She shut that train of thought down immediately, and it felt like being forced to surface—to breathe again—and being slammed back into reality. Just because Niua was an equal-opportunity flirt didn't mean she had any interest in following through with any woman, least of all with Mallory. She really shouldn't even be holding her this close.

But Niua had been awake when she'd wriggled into Mallory's space. She'd positioned Mallory's arms around her own body. She'd wanted to touch. And Mallory wasn't actually ever going to kiss her. Holding her wasn't about that. It was purely about offering and seeking a safe haven.

Mallory relaxed into the rhythm of the ship, breathing in time with the gentle movement of Niua's ribs. It had been a long time since anyone had sought her out in their sleep. She missed it. She missed having someone pressed into her side. She missed having someone to care about.

She didn't have enough information to know whether she *should* care.

But she did.

Whether it was wise or not.

Mallory didn't remember falling asleep. When she woke, she was alone. She blinked and rubbed her hands across her waist, hugging herself. There was no reason for the bed to feel empty. She was used to sleeping alone. She liked sleeping alone. Being alone did not mean being lonely. They were absolutely not the same thing.

So why did she feel like she didn't know where to place her arms without Niua on top of her?

She rolled to her side and realized Niua was in the washroom, the door open as usual, as if Niua, too, was used to living alone and wasn't in the habit of worrying about privacy. She'd changed into her borrowed T-shirt and too-tight shorts, and was leaning toward the mirror, applying bronze lipstick.

Mallory's lipstick.

At the sound of Mallory moving in the sheets, Niua glanced over at her, then went back to what she was doing.

Mallory lay there and stared.

"Is that my lipstick?" she finally asked.

"Mm-hmm." Niua pursed her lips together, evening out the color. "Is that all right?"

Now she asked?

Niua made faces at herself in the mirror, forming different shapes with her lips. "I didn't think you'd mind."

Her brazen self-confidence was admirable.

And annoying.

She was wearing Mallory's clothes. Sleeping in her cabin. Sleeping in her *bed*. All of which Mallory had invited her to do. No—*told* her to do. There were plenty of boundaries being crossed already.

The lipstick should not be the thing that threw her off balance.

"Hasn't anyone ever warned you about all the diseases you could catch from sharing makeup?" Which was not even remotely the real issue, but somehow that was what came blurting out of her mouth.

"I'm not worried," Niua said breezily.

"You should be."

Niua shot her a questioning, vaguely amused look.

Mallory twisted the sheets. As far as she knew, she wasn't infected with anything, but it was the principle of the thing.

Niua shrugged and went back to looking at herself in the mirror with childlike fascination. It was one of those unguarded moments that were completely at odds with the man-eater persona she projected in public. Somehow, she hadn't yet lost her sense of innocence and wonder. Trying on lipstick, caressing the sheets, enjoying a single bran flake as it dissolved on her tongue, watching Mallory spin the Rubik's Cube like Mallory was some kind of genius.

Those moments were awakening a yearning in Mallory's heart, making her want to cradle Niua in her arms and shelter her from the world's hurtfulness. Like she'd done for hours in the night before finally being overtaken by sleep.

Niua could obviously take care of herself, though. They'd both let down their guard in the dark, but now, in the light of day, it was time to be practical.

Niua replaced the lipstick cap with a click. She approached the bed and held out the tube. "Here."

Sharing makeup. They'd gone over this. "You keep it."

"But it's yours." Niua looked confused. She lowered her arm.

Mallory did need that lipstick. She couldn't replace it until they returned to shore, the salt air was brutal, and she'd forgotten to pack lip balm. If she wiped the end of the tube really well with a tissue, she could probably consider using it again.

After it had touched Niua's lips.

Gliding, shiny, slick…

Her lips tingled.

Why were they tingling? She was irritated, not…whatever this was.

She didn't want to think about sharing that lipstick.

She didn't want to think about kissing that lipstick off Niua's mouth.

Mallory pushed off the covers, swung off the bunk, and got to her feet. Time to get up and think about something else. Once she was out of this too-small cabin and busy with work, she'd be fine.

"Sorry," Niua said, giving up and placing the lipstick in the cabinet where she'd found it. "I was curious." She ran the tip of her tongue along her lower lip. Like she was tasting it. Like she honestly was curious, and not reflexively reverting to her flirtatious nonsense. "The texture is strange."

"Haven't you ever worn lipstick before?"

Niua shook her head in a noncommittal way that was neither a yes nor a no.

Mallory approached the washroom, hoping Niua would get the hint and switch places with her. "What made you decide to try it? Were your lips dry?"

"Not especially." Niua flattened herself against the door so Mallory could squeeze past.

Mallory hesitated. "Lucky you. Mine are chapped."

"Oh." Niua sounded surprised. They were standing practically on top of each other in the doorway, but neither of them moved. "Your lips peel?"

"Yours don't?"

"I suppose I must have strong skin."

"Strong skin." What a strange way to put it. The previous morning she'd claimed to have a strong stomach that could handle potentially contaminated water. What next? Strong bones that didn't bruise?

"Or I've adapted to my environment?"

Mallory needed to move past her, not stand there, awkwardly close, noticing that Niua had done a crap job on her upper lip and colored past the edge.

Instead, she reached out to fix the lipstick with her thumb.

What am I doing?

Niua watched, her pulse fluttering in her neck.

Mallory's hand was unsteady. She rested her fingers on Niua's jaw to anchor herself.

Niua's lips parted with a soft gasp.

She's going to think I want to kiss her.

Mallory smudged the bronze stickiness, stroking the edge of her lip, cleaning it up. Niua relaxed into her, her jaw pushing trustingly into Mallory's touch.

I shouldn't be touching her.

Niua was a flirt. She flirted with everyone, and Mallory refused to embarrass herself by believing this intriguing creature would actually want her. She lifted her thumb but hovered there, unable to pull away completely. The errant color was now on her own skin, evidence of what she'd done.

"All fixed," Mallory said, even though it wasn't, it was worse. Sure, Niua no longer looked like her fine motor skills had been inadequate to the task of doing her makeup on a tossing boat. Instead, she looked debauched, like her lipstick had started out perfect and then been kissed and licked until it smeared.

It was a good look on her. All messed up and wild like she'd looked that first day with her tangled wet hair. It suited her.

I shouldn't be staring at her mouth.

Niua swayed toward her like she wanted her to touch her again.

"You've never tasted lipstick?" Mallory's voice was nothing more than a broken whisper as she traced Niua's upper lip. "Not even on someone else?"

Niua's eyes fluttered shut as she reached for her with both hands and blindly ran her fingers through Mallory's hair.

Mallory shivered. There was something in the way Niua touched her that made her feel treasured, and that was almost more than she could take.

Because it wasn't real. Mallory wasn't precious to her. Mallory had never been precious to anyone, not for long. To be truly loved? That was probably never going to happen.

That wasn't what this was. Niua might want her, but wanting wasn't caring.

No matter how good it felt.

As if sensing Mallory's hesitation, Niua opened her eyes. She didn't pull back, though. She kept her hands right where they were and continued to sift through handfuls of Mallory's hair. Strands slid through her fingers in slow, hypnotic sweeps until they fell from her fingertips and she sank in again.

It felt like caring.

Like tenderness.

Like more.

They stood so close, breathing each other's air. It wasn't close enough.

Mallory touched her thumb to the corner of Niua's mouth.

"Mm." Niua's approving hum sounded like she'd been waiting for Mallory to do exactly this. She flicked her tongue and licked at Mallory's thumb.

A sharp pang of arousal hit Mallory low in the gut.

What am I doing?

She slid her thumb into Niua's mouth.

Like she had a right to.

Like she hadn't just been telling herself that sharing a tube of lipstick was too intimate and she didn't want to cross that line.

Now look what she was doing. What *they* were doing.

She's going to think...

Mallory couldn't finish the thought.

Niua closed on Mallory's thumb and licked, lingering on the spot where the lipstick was, getting it slick.

Mallory sucked in a breath. Niua's mouth was warm and wet and perfect, and the confident touch of her tongue made Mallory feel things she didn't think she'd feel from just this.

She's going to think I want her.

Niua reached again for Mallory's hair.

And she'll be right.

9

M allory was eager to see what the dredge would discover this time. A nice chunk of cold lava in her hands would give her something to focus on other than the memory of Niua's fingers massaging her scalp. Among other memories.

After Niua had let go and left Mallory alone in front of the washroom mirror, Mallory had raised her thumb slowly toward her mouth and watched herself in a daze.

Just one lick. Just to know the taste of Niua's tongue on her skin.

No. Mallory was here to work, not…whatever this was.

But the thought of not knowing had been unbearable. Not to the scientist in her, not to her ingrained curiosity, but to the part of her that *wanted*. She imagined doing it, and her abs clenched.

She'd given in.

And now she couldn't stop thinking about *that*, either.

Super helpful, Mallory. Really.

If only the dredge would start moving. Unfortunately, things were off to a slow start due to some unexplained delay involving two of the crewmembers who were needed to operate the thing. Courtland was scowling in the direction of the ship's interior and chatting with Niua as she spun the Rubik's Cube in her hands. Most of the scientists milled about aimlessly or gazed out to sea like passengers on a cruise ship, but Mallory stood dutifully with a small knot of colleagues in the cordoned-off waiting area even though they weren't required to stay there when the winch wasn't moving. Because she was waiting. Not because her location put her close—but not too close—behind Niua, where, coincidentally—

pathetically—Mallory could hear every word she said. Not because she couldn't keep away from her.

"Look how much I did," Niua said, showing Courtland the cube.

"It's only one side," Courtland said.

"I'm making progress."

"If that's what you call progress."

"It is."

Mallory couldn't see the cube from this angle, but she could tell from the way Niua's shoulders moved that she was twisting the cube some more, undiscouraged by Courtland's lack of enthusiasm.

"Nobody can solve that thing," Courtland said, his attention clearly wandering away to other activity on the deck.

Niua continued working the cube in silence. She could have contradicted him—she'd seen Mallory solve it twice—but she didn't. Good. If people were going to talk about her, Mallory wanted it to be for her research, not for a party trick.

Courtland glanced back at what Niua was doing and shook his head like she was wasting her time. "Remember to keep the children out of the way until it's time for the lolly scramble."

Niua turned and scanned the deck. When her gaze landed on Mallory, she paused.

That lipstick was still on her mouth.

Mallory didn't have any trouble maintaining a professional distance in front of their shipmates, but not staring? That, she was failing at.

She'd wanted to kiss her this morning. Last night, too. Maybe if she had, she wouldn't be obsessing about it now, imaging how good it would be.

Yeah, right. If they'd kissed, she'd be obsessing about it *more*.

"Please stay behind the rope." Niua tossed the reminder vaguely to everyone in the vicinity before turning back to Courtland. "Must they be corralled already? You haven't lowered the winch yet."

"We're preparing to lower it." He glowered into the distance. "We *will* be preparing to lower it once Giancarlo and Omar get their asses up here."

That certainly didn't sound imminent, and it was pointless to stand around waiting when there was an endless backlog of work waiting for her in the lab.

"Courtland," Mallory called out. "How much longer?"

"Not long."

"I'll believe it when I see it," one of the igneous petrologists grumbled. He stepped over the rope that was supposed to hem them in and lumbered off, carelessly knocking his empty bucket against everything in his path. The other men followed, leaving only Mallory behind the rope.

Should she wait?

"They get quite worked up about this, don't they?" Niua said to Courtland. "What's so important about these rocks?"

"What do I know?" Courtland said. "Mallory's standing right there. Ask her."

Niua found Mallory's gaze again and bit her lip.

Would Niua ask? If she really wanted to learn about Mallory's research, she'd already had plenty of chances to bring it up. So either she already knew exactly what they were studying—and was pretending ignorance—or she wasn't interested. If Mallory could figure out which one of those explanations was true, she'd be closer to understanding why Niua was on the ship.

Although it hardly seemed to matter anymore. Everyone treated Niua like part of the crew, like there was nothing strange about her presence at all. And Mallory wasn't any better. She liked her. It was hard to remember to be suspicious when the stowaway was the closest thing she had to a friend among all the scientists and crew who should have felt like friends, but didn't. To be honest, the unanswered questions that swirled around her were becoming more of an attraction than a deterrent.

"We're looking for volcanoes," Mallory said, inviting herself into their conversation when she couldn't stand it anymore. "It's hard to believe how little we know about what the seafloor looks like once we get away from shore."

The two-way radio clipped to Courtland's belt squawked. He turned away to listen to it.

Niua narrowed the gap between herself and Mallory until they were at a more comfortable speaking distance. "Less than you know about the surface of the moon, that's what Hudson told me."

More than we know about you.

Niua continued to approach until she was too close, really, for anyone watching not to guess they'd spent the night in each other's arms.

Mallory stiffened.

Niua ran her tongue thoughtfully along her upper lip. "Afraid of me?"

"No." Mallory was overreacting. Women could share personal space and no one looked twice. Women were supposed to be welcoming and nurturing and boundary-impaired—regardless of what that did to their ability to be taken seriously, regardless of whether it was even true to their actual personality.

Niua swayed toward her, obviously not bothering to fight the motion of the ship as it sent her forward. "What got you interested in volcanoes?"

"Um…" What was Niua doing? She wasn't going to pretend to accidentally fall on her, was she? Here? In front of everyone?

"They are rather interesting," Niua said, righting herself just in time. "All silent and mysterious."

"And unpredictable." Mallory considered taking a step back. "Not to mention violently dangerous."

"Is that what you love about them? The danger?"

"It's certainly one of the reasons we'd like to know where they are."

"Do they scare you?"

"A little."

"But you love them anyway."

"I want to understand them."

Niua raised her chin to speak directly into her ear. "Are you good at it?"

"I think so."

Too close, too intense, too tempting...

"Will you explain them to me?"

This time Mallory did step back. "That feels like a pickup line, not a real question."

Niua shook her head, eyes glinting. She looked amused. "I'll bet you've always had a scientific mind. I'm imaging you as a child with a rock collection in a cardboard box, all carefully labeled. I can see you being adorably earnest and sincere, taking the stones out and naming each one."

It was an easy guess. Didn't most kids do that sort of thing? With dolls or figurines or toy cars?

"Actually, it was a seashell collection." She'd shown it to everyone—whether they wanted to stand still long enough to listen to her ramble on about it or not. She hadn't learned yet that being earnest and sincere about unusual topics would get her labeled a weirdo. "I wanted to be a marine biologist."

Niua angled her body into the shelter of Mallory's shoulders and gently—affectionately—tangled her fingers in the leather cord hanging from Mallory's neck.

Mallory grasped Niua's wrist to stop her.

That meant Niua's forearm was trapped against Mallory's chest, which did nothing to stop Niua from continuing on her ill-advised journey and fishing Mallory's shark-tooth pendant out of her cleavage.

"Niua..." She could only hope anyone who noticed would assume they were trying to hear each other over the noise of the ship's engine and the wind.

Niua lowered her head and shook it so her hair cascaded forward and curtained her hand—and its position at Mallory's neckline—from view.

With a little effort, Mallory could put an end to this, but instead, she watched helplessly as Niua settled the shark's tooth on the outside of her work shirt. It felt ridiculously intimate. Niua was barely touching her, yet somehow Mallory felt her proximity shiver all the way through her.

"Marine biology." Niua flattened her palm over Mallory's heart. "I should have guessed."

"I know it's a cliché."

"Is it?"

The wind caught Niua's hair and blew it against Mallory's neck in a rough caress.

Another shiver overtook her, nerve-tingling and uncontrollable.

Mallory took a step back and released Niua's wrist. Niua lowered her arm in slow motion, seemingly reluctant to break contact. Mallory's heart hammered like she was at the bottom of a dive and it was time to turn around and leave because it was unsafe to stay any longer, no matter how much she wanted to. She liked it when Niua touched her. She loved it. But they were out in the open, and if she didn't put some distance between them, she was going to do something she shouldn't.

"My mother had a group of friends she'd invite over for lunch," Mallory said. "During their tarot card phase, when they were learning, they'd practice doing readings for each other. They dragged me into it, too. I'd shuffle the cards, I'd pick some out, and they'd tell me my future. Things like…I'd fall in love with a handsome blond guy, or do a lot of traveling, or…you know. I didn't mind." She really hadn't. She'd found tarot less embarrassing than trekking out to the cemetery on midnight ghost hunts and more fun than reading tea leaves. "So this friend of my mother's asked me what I wanted to be when I grew up, and I told her, and as I was picking a card, she told me that—" Was she really talking about this? She rarely told anyone about her childhood. "She told me that every little girl, if she wasn't dreaming about riding horses, wanted to be a marine biologist and communicate with dolphins." Mallory'd been a teenager—not a little girl—and she'd recognized a condescending laugh when she heard one. Her face had burned. "I wanted to explain it wasn't about wearing a cute glittery sequined dolphin sweatshirt and pretending I was a mermaid. I was serious. I wanted to tell her about the animals that grew the shells in my shell collection. I wanted to tell her how amazing it is that capelin—" She hesitated. She'd already shared more about herself than others usually wanted to hear. "Are you familiar with them?"

"Yes." Niua's eyes widened. "No?"

That was a strange reaction. But Niua looked like she was waiting for her to go on, so Mallory continued. "They're these fish we have in Canada that look like sardines. They have these tiny little brains, but they all know when to roll in with the tide to spawn, everyone together on a single night, everyone joining the group at the particular beach they've chosen. The waves are full of them, right up to the water's edge, everywhere, a chaos of slippery silver bodies, all laying their eggs where they'll sink between the beach pebbles, together. How do they know? How amazing is it that they know?"

"Strange how our bodies can do things by instinct that our conscious minds could never manage."

"So true," Mallory said. "It's magical. But it's science. They know it's time because they're reacting to the water's temperature and turbulence. I wanted to understand how biologists puzzled that out, how they knew it was the water conditions and not fish telepathy like my mother said, or some other kind of communication, or the pull of the full moon like my friends thought. Actually I knew it wasn't the moon, because anyone who paid attention could see the timing didn't match up. But my mother would have told me that studying the lives of fish would make people think I was strange." Explaining things to her parents—or the other adults in her life—or her friends—never ended well.

"I'm sorry she steered you away from something you loved."

"I didn't want anyone to think I was a predictable little girl with a predictable little-girl obsession." She'd wanted to be taken seriously, so when she saw dolphins had the opposite effect, she changed course. She shrugged. "It all worked out. I love geology. Eventually I had to specialize to get a job, but in theory, it has everything: biology, chemistry, physics, math...even fish, if they're fossilized."

"Even sharks." Niua's gaze flicked down to Mallory's pendant.

"Even the ocean. I'll never understand why the average person looks up at the stars and wonders what's out there, but when they encounter the ocean, they think the surface is the only interesting thing about it. They don't find it bizarre that we've never seen most of what's down there, that right here on earth there's this deep, dark, mysterious place we know hardly anything about. There's so much to learn. I could spend lifetimes out here."

"That long?" There was a wistful note in Niua's voice that made Mallory wonder if she was about to touch her again.

"What would you spend lifetimes learning about?" Mallory asked.

"Oh, I don't know."

"Too busy with your life of crime to explore other interests?"

Niua flashed her a secret smile, like Mallory's suspicions were a private joke they shared. "You truly don't regret giving up on marine biology? I know you said you're happy, but I can tell those capelin still have a place in your heart."

How could this person she barely knew see right through her? And get her to talk about things she did *not* talk about? Mallory cleared her throat, tight with emotions she didn't like to feel. "Sometimes it bothers me that I can still hear her voice. You know? That I cared what she thought. What anyone thought. That I wasn't strong enough to say, 'I like this stuff and you don't get to tell me I'm a stupid kid who doesn't know any better.'"

"Caring what another person thinks about you isn't a weakness."

Mallory swallowed. Her vision blurred.

"No one's born with a hard shell," Niua said gently. "And now you make your own decisions. You follow your own compass."

Niua was nicer to her than she deserved.

10

When Mallory returned to her cabin that night, Niua lay sprawled like a starfish faceup on top of the sheets, taking up the entire bed. The bedside reading light was on. Her eyes tracked Mallory's movements with an intensity that didn't look sleepy at all.

Mallory turned her back to her and changed into a spaghetti-strap sleepshirt and shorts. When she turned around again, Niua seemed to be taking up even more of the bed than before.

"Is there any room for me?"

Niua didn't budge. "Plenty of room."

"Where?" Not thinking too hard about what she was doing, Mallory crawled onto the bed and straddled her. Their legs touched, but she made sure no other part of her made contact. She planted her hands on either side of Niua's head. She'd created a standoff, and she didn't even know what kind of point she was trying to make.

Niua looked her up and down like she was looking forward to seeing what Mallory did next. "Found it?"

Mallory was tempted to position her knee between Niua's thighs, lean forward, and slide her leg up. But she just couldn't. If Niua was manipulating her...if Niua was analyzing her and knew that obvious, outright flirtation annoyed her...if Niua was calculating the best way to con her into bed as part of her master plan...then Mallory was going to regret letting down her guard. Again. She'd already lost track of how many times she'd allowed herself to forget she knew absolutely nothing about who this woman was, and it'd only been three days. "Scoot over."

"Or what?"

"Or I'll lie on top of you."

Niua licked her bottom lip like she was considering it. "That is quite the dilemma."

She should have known Niua would take that as encouragement. She could hardly blame her. Trapping her between her hands and knees wasn't exactly making it easy for her to get out of the way. This had been a bad idea.

Mallory swung over to one side of her, Niua wriggled in the opposite direction, and they both made room for each other until they were settled and lying on their backs like cozy sardines.

"This works, too," Niua said.

Mallory folded her hands behind her head. What now? Were they sleeping? The cabin was stifling. Outside, the night air would be cooler, but inside, there was only lukewarm air blowing in through the vent and the weak, inadequate breeze of her small fan. Sweat dampened her hair. "It's so warm in here."

"The fan is nice," Niua said.

"It's not enough. Aren't you sweltering?"

"I'll survive."

"I don't know if I will." Mallory rolled out of the bunk. "I'll go get ice."

Only after she was dressed in clothes she could be seen in public in and was on her way to the ice machine one deck up did she remember Niua was supposed to sleep on the floor. She wasn't going to kick her out of the bed, though. The first night, Mallory'd assumed the floor of her cabin was a step up from whatever hiding place Niua had been curling up in and therefore fine, but now, after the rough sea Niua had endured the night before, it would be unthinkable to exile her to the floor.

She returned with two plastic cups filled with water and ice cubes and a small bucket of ice for when they finished those. She clicked the bedside light to its dimmest setting and handed Niua one of the cups.

Niua propped herself up on one elbow. She tipped the cup to her mouth and caught an ice cube. It looked like she was moving it around in her mouth.

Mallory averted her gaze. She didn't want to stare. She gulped down her water and wedged her cup between the mattress and the bulkhead, changed back into her sleepwear, and got into bed with a minimum of *this-bed-is-too-small-why-are-we-doing-this-sorry-your-leg-is-in-the-way* unavoidable touching. She lay down beside her, kicked at the duvet until it slid to the floor, and pressed an ice cube to the pulse point at the base of her neck. The cold burned. Then it felt good.

Niua showed off her own ice cube, its edges now softened, balancing on her tongue. "You naw dwinking it?" she drawled, the ice garbling her words.

Mallory made herself face the ceiling and nowhere else—because why did she keep looking at Niua's mouth, there was no reason for this—and glided the ice up and down the front of her neck, keeping it moving so no one spot went numb. Meltwater trickled down the side of her neck and down the valley between her breasts. "If you cool the artery, it tricks you into thinking your whole body's cooling off."

"Why resort to tricks"—the ice clacked against the back of Niua's teeth—"when you brought all this ice?"

"This is what I wanted it for."

Niua closed the distance between them and pressed her own ice cube to Mallory's shoulder. While her ice cube was in her mouth.

Mallory jerked in surprise. Her skin flushed. "Is that a kiss?" she asked stupidly.

Niua slid the strap of Mallory's top off her shoulder and pushed it down her arm, out of the way.

Mallory watched helplessly and let her.

Without raising her head, Niua guided the ice in a circle over Mallory's shoulder, then migrated toward her breastbone. It was a very open-mouthed kiss, but it *was* a kiss. Her lips were absolutely touching her. There wasn't just meltwater on her skin; there was also saliva.

Which did not help Mallory cool off.

Because she liked it. She liked the intrusion into her personal space and the heat of Niua's mouth and the cold of the ice and the ocean-like scent of her hair. Mallory was used to being the pursuer, not the pursued, but the short-circuiting of her brain left no doubt how profoundly good this felt.

Did she trust it, though?

"You don't need to do this to convince me to let you stay in the bed," Mallory said.

Reluctantly, Niua pulled off. She sucked the remaining sliver of ice back into her mouth and visibly swallowed. Licked her lips.

Mallory needed more water. And ice. And willpower.

"Mm." Niua touched the pad of one finger to a spot between Mallory's collarbones. She traced circles in the moisture, rubbing it into Mallory's skin. She seemed riveted by the sight. "That's not what this is." With her other hand, she pushed up the hem of Mallory's shirt, exposing her waist.

Mallory caught her hand and stopped her. "Are you trying to seduce me?"

"I…"

Mallory sat up. Adjusted her shirt. She wished she could close her eyes and let whatever was going to happen, happen, but she needed to be sure Niua wasn't going to regret this. For both their sakes. "I'm not particularly comfortable with this dynamic."

Niua's expression clouded. "What dynamic?"

"You're completely dependent on us."

"What? On you? No, I'm not."

"On the captain," Mallory said. "On the goodwill of the crew."

Niua sat up so they were eye to eye. "I can take care of myself."

"How? We're days away from shore. You're stuck on this ship. If the captain decides he doesn't like you—if I decide I don't like you—we could make your life uncomfortable." She remembered how Niua had checked the latch on the cabin door. "We could lock you in a cabin."

Niua pulled away and balanced at the edge of the bed, ready to take flight, then seemed to change her mind and flopped back down. "You promised you wouldn't, and I believe you."

"Maybe you shouldn't."

"Shouldn't that be for me to decide?"

If their situations were reversed, Mallory would behave the same way: Make light of the threat. Make sure the enemy didn't sense her vulnerability. "Are you pretending you're not worried?"

"What dastardly plans are you contemplating, then? To starve me to death?"

"Of course not. But I could."

"You wouldn't."

Niua was bluffing. She had to be. She was smarter than this. "Can't you see the position you're in? You're sleeping in my sheets, wearing borrowed clothes, eating our food. You have an incentive to stay on my good side." Niua had reason to flatter her and even to kiss her…and not because she honestly liked her or wanted her. The possibility turned Mallory's stomach.

Niua softened. "Nothing I did was done to stay on your good side." She settled closer to her. The bunk wasn't big enough that there'd ever been all that much physical distance between them, but now there was less. "It's kind of you to worry about me. Believe me, though. I could survive on my own."

"How?"

"I…I could…" Niua obviously had to think about it. Precisely Mallory's point. "I could steal a lifeboat."

"Without anyone noticing?"

"Yes."

Doubtful. "And then what? Wait for another ship to rescue you?"

"Yes."

"You can't honestly believe that."

"You worry too much, *kleine Maus*."

Mallory heaved an exasperated sigh. She admired Niua's self-confidence. She did. "I worry the right amount." At least she did when she had enough data to understand the situation. Which, in this case, she didn't. She didn't know anything. Because Niua wouldn't tell her anything. So if Niua insisted this was okay, then Mallory should believe her. Mallory traced Niua's bracelet along its spiral path up her forearm, touching her without touching skin.

Niua brushed a strand of hair out of Mallory's eyes with a tenderness Mallory didn't know what to do with. Because it felt real.

She wanted this to be real.

Yes, caution was warranted. But she wanted to be brave. She wanted to trust herself. She wanted to believe she could fall for a woman who wouldn't make her regret it. Because she was already falling for her. Already half in love with her. Mallory didn't do casual.

And she wasn't going to start by letting Niua give her a coward's nickname. "Tell me you did not just call me a little mouse."

"A *cute* little mouse?" Niua pursed her lips and squinted, obviously thinking hard as she searched for a way to spin this. "An *understanding* little mouse."

Mallory sucked in her cheeks, trying hard not to laugh. Niua looked so earnest. Mallory took Niua's hand and kissed her fingertips to take the sting out of her words. "Thanks a lot."

"It's meant to be nice."

"I certainly hope so."

Niua relaxed into a mischievous grin. "You prefer to be *le grand méchant loup*?"

"The large…" Mallory collaborated with researchers across the globe and could often guess the meaning of the titles of the foreign-language papers they published, but that was because scientific words were frequently similar around the world. *Vulkan, volcan, vulcano, vulcão, wulkan, vulkaan*… She didn't need to be multilingual to understand those. But Niua wasn't suggesting she call her a volcano, so she was at a loss.

"The big bad wolf," Niua translated, waggling her eyebrows and curling her fingers into pretend claws.

Why did she look adorable doing that? Ugh. Because everything she did made her look adorable, that's why.

Mallory gave up and pulled her into her arms so they were face to face, Niua's hip pressed into Mallory's side. "It's not that I want you to not trust me. I just need to know that if we're going to do...this...it's because you want to, not because I'm standing between you and your ability to survive."

Niua tucked her chin onto Mallory's shoulder. "This?"

She felt so good there. "Yeah." The tension of the day—and of this whole situation—began to unwind. Mallory's lungs relaxed; her breath deepened. The rush of oxygen made her dizzy.

"That's thoughtful of you." Niua turned her face into Mallory's neck. Her hair smelled like the ocean, and its loose strands were everywhere, touching Mallory's jaw and sweeping across her bare arm.

Mallory shivered.

"Thoughtful, but unnecessary," Niua continued, pressing closer.

"If you say so."

"I'm not scared of you," Niua said, her lips moving against Mallory's skin.

Didn't seem like it.

"Trying to"—Mallory's voice cracked—"kiss the computer passwords out of me?" She'd meant it as a joke, but it wasn't a joke, not really. If this was a trick to steal information out of her...well, she'd find out soon enough. For now, she was pretty sure she didn't care.

Niua shook her head. The motion made her hair move back and forth like a caress. It felt almost more intimate than the touch of her mouth. "Not today."

Mallory laughed. That was evasive enough that she actually believed her.

And now Niua was one step closer to joining the long list of women who'd gotten past Mallory's walls only to decide there was something wrong with her.

Kimberly had complained Mallory never had time for her and

cared only about work. Tanisha said they spent too much time together and she needed space. Cindy Number One said Mallory's diving was dangerous. Cindy Number Two said her diving was an obsession—and the way she said the word *obsession* made it clear it was not a good thing. Samar was better, because she shared her love of freediving, but complained Mallory's sex drive was too low. Valencia complained her sex drive was too high. Noelle accused her of being too intellectual, Elaine said she was too intense, Mimi said she never wanted to do anything fun, and Cindy Number Three said she didn't think Mallory liked people—and seeing as how she herself was a person, she was leaving.

Mallory had loved each of them in her own way—or at least tried to be open to the possibility of loving them—but it was never enough. One of these days, it was going to become too depressing to even try anymore.

After Niua.

After Mallory tried—again—to make it work with a woman she couldn't figure out, because the straightforward, easy-to-understand ones didn't intrigue her. She loved puzzles, and a puzzle was exactly what Niua was.

Without warning, the ship plunged into a wave's trough. They held each other tightly, seeking stability in each other's bodies.

"Straddle me," Mallory suggested. It would help them balance. No other reason.

But Niua was already wedging her hip into Mallory's body more securely, knees stacked one on top of the other, legs folded at her side in the classic mermaid pose. "Oh." Niua glanced down at herself like she wasn't sure how she'd gotten there. She settled in even more firmly. "Not yet."

She smoothed her palm over Mallory's head and drew the tips of her hair to her lips. Mallory couldn't feel the kiss, but it made her shiver nevertheless.

Niua took a fresh ice cube and held it to the back of her own neck. She closed her eyes and brought the ice around to the hollow of her throat until it began to drip, then drew it downward, following the water's path to her cleavage. Wet splotches appeared on the neckline of her borrowed tank top. And lower.

Mallory couldn't look away.

Tension swirled between them like ocean currents, promising to push them together and sweep them under, a force they could resist for only so long before they were overpowered.

Niua pulled her tank top off over her head.

She was beautiful. All women were beautiful, but even in the dim, unflattering artificial light of the cabin's reading lamp, Niua was not like anyone Mallory had ever managed to get into her bed. She had a swimmer's shoulders, the solid biceps of a woman who needed to be strong to survive, and vulnerable breasts that looked like they'd never been subjected to the pull of gravity. She'd expected to see bruises from being thrown across the cabin floor, but her skin was unmarred.

Mallory lifted her gaze to Niua's face. Niua's eyes, black as a seal's, seemed almost feral. They didn't flash with the timid interest of her first girlfriend or sparkle with the eager enthusiasm of her second one or even glimmer with the tired wariness of her tenth. When she held her gaze and really looked—sank deep into the unbearable intimacy of it—there was a glint of obsidian guarding something ageless and terrible that Niua didn't share with anyone.

Mallory liked that about her. Mallory didn't want innocent or naïve or easily discouraged, and Niua wasn't any of those things. Niua gave the impression that she was aware of the darkness, yet unafraid.

This time, when Niua pulled up on Mallory's shirt, Mallory not only let her, but helped her tug it off. When it was past her face and off her arms and had landed on the floor, Niua smiled. Not the hard, dangerous smile she'd given the captain or the manipulative one she used to get what she wanted. A new smile. A private smile, soft and full of promise.

Mallory was sure she was smiling, too. It had been a long time since she'd felt like this.

Niua ran her hands down Mallory's sides to her waist and pulled her in until their upper bodies were flush. Mallory clung to her, soaking in the dizzying sensation of being skin to skin.

Niua rose to her knees, bringing Mallory with her and lowering her onto her back, all the while remaining kneeling at her side. Mallory made a small noise of protest. She wanted to feel Niua's weight on top of her.

"I'm coming back," Niua murmured. She reached for another ice cube and held it just above Mallory's breastbone, hovering, waiting, a silent question in her eyes.

"Yeah." Mallory's voice sounded breathy. Wrecked already, and their tongues hadn't even touched.

Niua pressed the ice to her skin.

Mallory bucked at the contact, but Niua was already moving on, gently sliding the ice between Mallory's breasts, tracing lazy patterns over her curves, making her squirm. She was careful, and that was why it felt good, wasn't it? Niua was shaking, but controlled—controlled enough to pay attention to how Mallory was reacting and adjust her path accordingly. Slow, but intent. And obviously into it.

Very, very into it.

Niua mapped her body like she couldn't believe she was lucky enough to be allowed to touch her and worried she'd never be allowed to again. Like it was essential to learn the topography of her body, travel her entire length, memorize every dip and swell. Like Mallory was precious. Like Niua wasn't going to wake up tomorrow and decide she didn't like her enough to stick around, after all. Like Mallory was more than a convenient body.

It was embarrassing how much Mallory wanted that.

The ice left swirling trails through the sweat glistening on her skin, proof that Niua had explored her, touched her, made her shiver. Had anyone ever traced the angle of her lowest rib or the divot of her navel? Found the place under her arm that ached whenever she sat at a desk too long? Mallory'd always dreamed of this—yearned for this—and never found it: a woman who touched her like she was the only thing that mattered. Afterward, when this was over, no one would ever be able to find a place on her body that wouldn't remind her that Niua had claimed her there first.

"I can't get enough of you." Niua lowered her head and kissed all the way across her collarbone, bringing with her the scent of sun-baked stones, algae, and brine—which might be a strange thing to find appealing, but absolutely did it for her. "You taste amazing." She shifted her weight and dropped her hips onto her.

Mallory was going to break apart. She gripped Niua's waist as low as she could reach and arched beneath her.

Niua licked her way back with a quiet, appreciative moan, her bottom lip grazing Mallory's skin, barely a kiss at all.

Better than a kiss.

Niua lingered at the base of her neck and looked up at her with half-lidded eyes. Dazed. Lust-drunk. She was diving in too fast, and she was letting Mallory see it. And all Mallory wanted to do was dive in after her.

"I should have known you'd be like this," Mallory said.

"Like what?"

"Reckless." Careful with the woman she was with, and not careful at all with her own heart.

Niua scooted up so their foreheads touched. "Am I in danger?"

Mallory wanted to say no, she'd never hurt her, she'd protect her, she was safe. But she couldn't say that, could she? Even if it felt true. She had to be sensible. With their foreheads pressed together, she helplessly shook her head.

Niua pressed a kiss to Mallory's cheek, and it felt like the most natural thing in the world for Mallory to turn and meet her lips. Niua was waiting for her, chasing her, rumbling at the back of her throat with pleasure. Mallory's breath caught. Plenty of women had kissed her with confidence; Niua kissed her with certainty. As if she knew they were right for each other. As if she'd already decided this relationship was going to work out. To know that Niua wanted her... It felt better than any physical touch. She leaned in and tasted Niua again, melting into her like the ice melted on their skin.

Niua settled more firmly on top of her, anchoring them both. Mallory rocked up into her. They licked into each other's mouths, seeking connection, asking for more. Yes. This. You. A tide of desire picked her up and tossed her until the world spun and she didn't know which way was up, until she didn't understand anything except this kiss. This endless, fathomless kiss.

$$\infty$$

Niua was in so deep she wasn't sure she could find her way out.

Being in love ought to make her feel safe. Being in love ought to mean there'd be someone who'd defend her when she was threatened and support her when she was weak. Being in love ought to mean she could relax, because the burden of staying vigilant was shared.

Niua was not falling in love with Mallory.

Not yet.

It wouldn't be safe.

Mallory couldn't protect her when she didn't know what the threat was. And Niua wouldn't tell her, because Mallory *was* the threat. Mallory tempted Niua to take unnecessary, ill-considered risks. Being around her was exhilarating—and foolish.

And futile. Because it wasn't real. Mallory didn't know her; she knew only what Niua allowed her to see. The acceptable parts.

Niua could lie to herself and pretend that was enough. With most people, it was. With Mallory, though…

She buried her face in Mallory's shoulder. When a man told her he liked her or he wanted her or he loved her, she didn't wonder if it was true. She *knew* it was a lie. It was her magic, turning his head. But when a woman said such things, or kissed her like she meant it, Niua couldn't help but hope her affection was real. And it *was* real…up to a point. The point where the woman realized she'd fallen in love with an illusion. A body that was less—and more—than it seemed. A life that didn't exist. Century after century, when the illusion shattered, they had recoiled in fear, in disgust, in betrayal.

She'd tried to bury those memories, but they were always there, lurking in the depths of her subconscious. She was the goddess's memory keeper, after all. She was incapable of forgetting.

And equally incapable of giving up hope.

Or of *not* diving in headfirst.

No matter what disappointment lay ahead, no matter how much it would hurt when Mallory eventually pushed her away, for now, while she had the chance, she wanted to bask in the glow of Mallory's desire and enjoy the comfort of their connection.

Heartache could come later, when she was alone again.

Niua pressed kisses into Mallory's skin everywhere she could reach: her cheekbone, the back of her earlobe, her jaw, the underside of her chin, the crease of her elbow, the inside of her wrist. She needed to touch her everywhere. Needed her.

She nuzzled Mallory's neck and breathed her in, pulling her scent deeply into her lungs, letting it melt the cold, frozen core of her sexuality, her true sexuality, the part she instinctively suppressed while her man-eater self—a weapon she kept always at the ready—was all anyone could see. Mallory had figured out that beneath her aggressive flirting lay a heart that wanted something else. Perhaps Niua had shown it to her, even. She was certainly showing her now, finding her mouth and kissing her like she didn't ever want to stop.

One night was not going to be enough. Twenty-five more wouldn't be, either, even if she could spare them, which she absolutely could not. She'd allow herself tonight, and the following day, and one more night after that. Then she'd have to go. She pushed that thought away. Mallory was here, warm and happy and gasping at her touch, and Niua wanted nothing but to lose herself in the perfect, fleeting joy of it.

Wordlessly, they rocked, fitting their curves together, angling for contact, an easy puzzle with more than one solution. Each slide of their bodies felt better than the last. Time stretched and thinned like a horizon they could never reach. She had no sense of how long they kissed or how much of the night remained. She floated, adrift in a sea where nothing mattered but entwining herself with this perfect soul and making them both forget they'd ever known what it was to exist apart.

11

At the end of her shift, Niua found Mallory in her usual laboratory standing alone at a long table that stretched nearly the entire length of the space, her head bent in concentration over—what else?—a rock, holding it close to her face and examining it through a hand lens.

Niua cleared her throat. Mallory raised her head, and her studious, closed-off expression transformed into something friendlier. She made a notation and set the rock down in a labeled plastic tub overflowing with a jumble of other rocks.

"What are you doing here?" Mallory asked.

"My shift is over."

"It is?" Mallory frowned at her computer, as if it was the machine's fault she hadn't noticed the time.

"Yours is over as well."

"I'm not done," Mallory said tightly, but her *leave-me-alone* attitude wasn't convincing. "I still have this entire group to do."

Niua circled the table and stood at Mallory's back, resting her chin on Mallory's shoulder to peer down at the array of rocks spread out on the table. Mallory reached behind herself without turning and pulled Niua close. Niua pressed her front to Mallory's back, fitting their bodies together.

"What are you working on?" Niua asked.

"I'm just taking a quick look to make sure we know what we're finding. If we see anything interesting and want to follow a lead, we need to know while we're in the vicinity, before the ship moves on. And if we don't like what we're seeing, we can change course."

"Can I help?"

"I don't think so. These rocks need to be sorted, but they'll all look the same to you."

"Could you teach me?" It didn't look that interesting, but Niua firmly believed the most interesting and beautiful things were the ones whose allure wasn't obvious on the surface.

"It would take too long."

Mallory was undoubtedly right, so Niua tried not to feel disappointed. "Then perhaps I won't help with the sorting." She bumped her knees into the backs of Mallory's thighs. "My help could be motivational."

Mallory leaned backward and relaxed into Niua's body. She may have swayed. And not because the ship pitched. "Not helping."

"Work faster, *tortuga*," Niua whispered into the tempting spot behind her ear. "Once you're done, I'll lure you out of the laboratory to do something just as wildly fun as examining pieces of the ocean floor, only much more private."

"I wonder what that could be."

"I realize it's hard to imagine anything as fun as science."

"It really is."

"But I'm sure I'll think of something."

Mallory wriggled into her in a promising manner, but let out a regretful sigh. "I need to work."

"So…work." Niua released her to pick out a chunky, good-sized lava stone from the large bucket at their feet and held it out. "These are the unsorted ones?"

"Uh-huh."

Niua frowned into the bucket. "You were right about them all looking the same."

"I'm not saying they're *not* the same. They could be. We dredged a small area, so it may be safe to assume the haul is approximately isotropic—you know, consistent." Mallory gently took the rock from her and returned it to the bucket. "But I'll need to check to be sure. Even though the very act of sampling is one giant assumption."

Mallory resumed her routine with the hand lens, and Niua stayed and watched her for a while. When it became clear she wasn't going to ask her to leave, Niua repositioned herself at Mallory's back, wrapped her arms around Mallory's waist, widened her stance to trap Mallory's legs between her feet, and once again molded their bodies together.

"Mm," Niua hummed happily.

"I thought you were going to let me work," Mallory murmured.

"I am letting you work."

Niua nudged Mallory's backside with an instinctual undulation of her hips. A swimmer's movement. If not for gravity, the force of it would have floated their legs up and propelled them both into a lazy, sensual somersault. It wasn't even sexual…not really.

Not until Mallory made a sound that might have been the start of an only partially swallowed moan…and then studied the rock beneath her lens as if nothing had happened.

Mallory said blandly, "If the dredged material is isotropic, we have to ask, how approximately? How good is the resolution? Do we need more samples closer together? Or could they be farther apart? How much are we kidding ourselves?"

Niua contemplated the nape of Mallory's neck. It looked kissable.

"Sorry," Mallory said. "You don't want to hear me ramble on about this."

Definitely kissable.

Lickable.

"If that's your tactful way of saying you think I don't understand what you're talking about, don't worry." She might not have caught every word, but that was for a different reason. "It's not going over my head."

"Are you sure?" Mallory set her rock down on the table instead of placing it in one of the tubs, as if she didn't want to move too far and make Niua think she wanted her to let go.

"Am I sure I understand that surveys inherently fail to detect complexity? Of course." Niua rubbed Mallory's shoulders. "This is what's wrong with your charts."

Mallory tipped her head back and rested it on Niua's shoulder. "Which you're not supposed to have access to."

"You measure the sea's depth at Point A and at Point B and draw a lovely straight line between them and color the whole area deep blue because it must all be the same. Then you're surprised when you run aground on a reef you had no idea lurked beneath that line."

"Or get hit by molten lava and frozen glass spewing from a volcano that's about to breach the surface as you sail right over it," Mallory agreed. "Although if that happened to me, I'd be squealing with excitement."

"If you survived," Niua said darkly, her face in Mallory's hair.

Mallory turned to kiss her jaw. "Aw, you're worried about me."

"You wouldn't be so excited if you were caught in a belch of toxic volcanic gas and suffocated."

Mallory angled to reach the underside of her jaw and licked, clearly not taking her seriously.

Niua leaned appreciatively into her touch and sank a hand into Mallory's hair. "Or if, deep underwater, a gas bubble one hundred meters across pushed the ocean's surface upward as it expanded, and created a tower of water that rose ominously over your head, and then the bubble burst, and the sea collapsed with it, and it swallowed your ship and dragged you down to your doom, so fast that you disappeared before you could radio a distress call."

"Where'd you learn so much about death by volcano?" Another kiss. "That's not common knowledge."

"You know it happens."

"Yeah, but...it's really just rumor. I mean, obviously ships disappear. But we don't know what happened. There are no witnesses."

That you know of. Niua suppressed a shudder. "The danger in pretending those carefully drawn lines are correct is ignored, because no one wants ugly blank white squares on their map marked *we're not certain...*"

"We'll never be able to map everything."

"Or *data unavailable...*"

"Experienced navigators understand the limitations of the data."

"Or *here be dragons.*"

Despite the talk of lurid disasters, Mallory laughed, that wonderful laugh of recognition that happened when two people understood each other so well that the joy of it bubbled up and couldn't be contained.

"Because that," Niua finished, "would mar their lovely blue drawing."

"I'm impressed." Mallory reached for Niua's hand and pressed her lips to her knuckles in a slow, appreciative kiss.

"That's why this ship is named the *Sea Monster, n'est-ce pas?* Because it explores the blank places—the sea dragons' realm—on your charts?"

"You're scarier than you let on. More intelligent."

Not intelligent enough to leave.

Mallory kissed her way across her hand from one knuckle to the next. "I think you want people to underestimate you."

The observation could have been unsettling, but Niua didn't mind it, not when she was dizzy with pleasure from the feel of Mallory's mouth and the warmth of her breath.

Mallory's lips moved across her skin, words and kisses blurring together. "I get that. It's safer."

It was. It was easier to hide in plain sight when she didn't give anyone a reason to search beneath the surface.

"You're brave," Mallory said. "You have to be, to be here on your own, doing whatever it is you're doing. But there are certain risks you're willing to take and others you're not. You're strategic. Which is smart." She interlaced their fingers. It felt like a promise.

Heat washed through her, wild and welcome. Mallory didn't know her secret, but she was starting to know *her*. There was no other feeling in the world like the feeling of being known. It was terrifying, and it was a relief, and goddess help her, she wanted more.

"Will we see each other again? After this?" Mallory squeezed her hand like she was afraid of the answer and didn't want to let her go.

"I…"

"Where do you live?"

"All over," Niua said. "You?" It was pointless to ask. They were never going to see each other again. But it would be nice to think of Mallory living out her days in Tasmania or Mauritius or the Canary Islands, where, years from now, Niua might find an uninhabited stretch of shoreline, sun herself on a rock, imagine Mallory relaxing on a similar rock, and remember.

"I'm working in Australia. Perth. South of there. The university has a strong marine geology program and maintains a field outpost away from the city where students can do research outdoors from our own boats."

"Didn't you say you were Canadian?"

Mallory gave her an odd look. "Didn't you say you lived all over? How many times have you moved?"

"I've lost count." Which was true. She reached for a plausible follow-up. "I assume others are more rooted to one place." Memories tumbled together and aligned in new patterns. "This outpost wouldn't happen to be near a museum of marine archaeology, would it?"

"It would. There's one associated with the university. Have you been?"

"I've heard of it." Thought of it. Dreamed of it. "Is it near the water?"

"That's the one."

"Will you show me? On a map?"

"Later?"

"Sure." Niua rested her forehead on Mallory's shoulder and inhaled her scent. She wished she could stay like this forever.

"I want to keep seeing you," Mallory said, stroking her thumb over Niua's hand. "You're avoiding telling me where you live, so I think that means you're going to say no, but is there any way we could?"

"I don't know," she mumbled into Mallory's collarbone.

"Can I have your number? If you think maybe…somehow…"

"I don't have one of those."

"You don't have a phone?"

"I prefer not to be enslaved by technology." Niua had been using that line for centuries. It was always applicable, no matter what the gadget of the day was. Whether it was a timepiece small enough to fit in one's pocket or a ship-to-shore radio, there was always a certain segment of the population who distrusted the latest advances.

"The back-to-nature type, eh?"

Niua nodded, rubbing her forehead into Mallory's neck.

"I don't believe you. You've been hassling the geophysicists for days like the worst kind of technogeek. There is no way—" Mallory stopped herself. "Okay, you're being cautious, and that's good. I even warned you to be cautious. So…okay. But if you ever want to visit me? After we reach port? I'd love that."

"I…" Niua evaded the truth all the time with very few qualms, but this time, it hurt. "I'd like to. I don't know if I'll be able to."

Mallory didn't pull away. If anything, she seemed to lean closer, answering Niua's unspoken need. "I'll try to convince you to make the effort."

If only it were that simple.

12

The next afternoon, Mallory stood on the trawl deck with the usual crowd waiting for the dredge to be pulled up. The sun blazed ruthlessly overhead in a cloudless sky; there was no wind to blow away the smell of diesel fuel.

Niua stood inattentive watch over the scientists from her position on the opposite site of the rope that was supposed to keep them corralled. She grumbled at the Rubik's Cube and twisted it to move a corner piece into position, which displaced another corner she'd already done.

"Want me to teach you how to protect that corner you lost?" Mallory asked, her fingers itching for something to do.

"No, thanks," Niua said. "I think I almost see it."

With a clank of the winch, the dredge began its return trip to the surface. Mallory and the other scientists edged closer to the rope, eager to catch their first glimpse of the latest haul.

The cable spooled up and up and up, pulling the dredge through the ocean's depths. It shuddered. Stopped. The men operating the winch swore.

The scientists froze. "What happened?" someone said.

"It's stuck," someone else answered.

"Obviously," growled the man beside her.

Mallory crossed her arms in annoyance. She watched the cable as if its stillness might be an optical illusion induced by the intense heat of the tropical sun bending light through the air, and if she stared hard enough, maybe she'd see it was really moving. The alternative was that the cable had caught on a rock or gotten itself wrapped around a protrusion in the undersea landscape. They could lose hours while the crew tried to free it. If they managed to free it at all.

Omar and Giancarlo were already reversing the direction of the winch, feeding the cable some slack as Courtland peered over the edge and communicated over his two-way radio with the captain.

Niua moved to Mallory's side, the cube still clenched in her hand. "What's going on?"

"The cable got caught. They'll try to unhook it. Move the ship in reverse and hope that works. If it doesn't, it'll take longer. They'll have to maneuver back and forth and try to find an angle that'll disentangle it."

The ship began to move.

"Can they see what they're doing down there?" Niua asked.

"With video, you mean? No. You've seen us take measurements and collect samples. We don't need visuals for that."

"There are no underwater cameras at all?"

"They wouldn't help in this situation anyway, because when the dredge scrapes the bottom, it makes a mess with all the sediment it stirs up. A camera would be blind."

"But they'll be able to free the dredge by feel?"

"I hope so."

Niua spun the Rubik's Cube uselessly, scrambling the side she'd already solved. "What happens if they can't?"

"They cut it loose. What else can they do?"

"And abandon it at the bottom of the sea."

Not anyone's preferred option. If they lost the dredge, did they even have another one? Mallory didn't know. She had a backup plan—there were other kinds of data she could collect if the original plan had to be scrapped due to weather or equipment failure—but it would be a huge disappointment to have to switch gears.

"They know what they're doing," Mallory said.

There was nothing she could do but wait.

∞

The dredge remained stuck, so Mallory went down to the rock lab to catch up on some work. She wasn't done analyzing earlier hauls, and that could keep her busy for hours.

She found Jasvinder and Wes in there looking at samples under their microscopes, but someone had cleared another one of the tables, so there was plenty of room for her. They both glanced up and said hello when she came in, then returned to their microscopes.

"Were you awake when that monster wave passed us?" Jasvinder asked Wes.

"When was this?" Wes said.

"Four o'clock this morning," Jasvinder said.

"I was asleep. Were you on shift?"

"I was."

"Then why are you still working? Go to bed."

"I take my work seriously."

Wes elbowed him. "Are you implying I don't?"

"Sleep is for people who don't make great scientific breakthroughs."

"Save it for someone who believes your bullshit," Wes said. "If you saw this wave, that means you were outside on deck, which means you weren't here in the lab, working."

"I was taking a break," Jasvinder protested. "While working."

Wes snorted. "And saw this wave."

"You should've seen it. It was huge!"

"Just the one?"

"Just the one. Came out of nowhere and then went along on its merry way."

"It would be exciting if it was related to a volcanic eruption," Mallory said.

Wes frowned like she'd barged in on a private conversation—which, okay, maybe she had—then turned back to his microscope. "Any volcanoes around here would be too deep below the surface to create a big wave."

"It's not impossible," Mallory said. There was research on this that Wes obviously wasn't aware of, but she'd only sound like a jerk if she mentioned it. "We hardly know anything yet about what's down there."

"We know enough to know it wasn't a volcano," Wes said.

"I thought about praying," Jasvinder said, "and I'm not the kind of person who prays."

"Couldn't have been that special if this is the first I'm hearing about it," Wes said. "Everyone would be talking about it."

"It was dark," Jasvinder said. "There weren't a lot of people out there to see it."

"The guys on the bridge would've seen it for sure," Wes said.

"I bet Vomit Boy turned green," Wes said.

"You mean Hudson?" Jasvinder said.

"Yeah."

"No idea."

With a sigh, Mallory gave up and focused on her rocks.

Jasvinder and Wes weren't in the mood to talk science with her. They were gossiping, and they didn't feel like including her. So what? It didn't matter. Some people were collegial and friendly with everyone, even those they'd never be friends with outside of work. Others weren't, and she'd had plenty of practice working with those kinds of people. She'd actually been getting along fine with Jasvinder since the beginning of the expedition, and she barely knew Wes, and it wasn't their fault if the conversation triggered memories of meetings and conferences and research collaborations where being overlooked did—very much—matter.

As a young adult beginning her career, she'd imagined the scientific community would be everything her childhood wasn't. Truth would be something to discover, rather than something you were taught. Ideas would be valued based on their scientific merit, not on the status of the person who voiced them. Anyone who was an outsider—due to age, race, gender, nationality, education, or professional background—would be listened to with just as much respect as an established insider would be. Diverse theories would be sought out, because scientists were explorers, and how could they learn anything new if they weren't open-minded?

Reality had been a disappointment.

Sure, everyone *said* they welcomed innovation, but when a hypothesis contradicted someone's life's work, it stood no chance. Slight variations on accepted doctrine were considered intriguing; ideas that were too different were ignored or mocked. Human nature hadn't changed much since the days when men were denounced as heretics for suggesting the earth was not flat.

Mallory's research wasn't on the fringe—she was firmly enough entrenched in the mainstream to have her grant proposals approved and her research published in respected journals—yet she always felt like she was watching her colleagues through a door, never inside their circle where she could really be heard, never enthusiastically welcomed into exciting conversations. Some days, that hurt. Other days, it was simply the cost of doing the work she loved. On the worst days, it made her question whether she really did love her research and whether it was worth it.

Her upbringing had taught her not to challenge authority, not to question the way things were done, not to voice her own thoughts—and it'd convinced her she never wanted to live that way again. Science should have been the answer. But science, and society itself, turned out not to be so different from the world she'd escaped.

Two hours later, the dredge remained stuck. Niua took advantage of the lull to slip away and track down Daphne, the ship's marine mammal observer. She was easy to spot: she was the one on the upper deck with her binoculars trained on the water. As Niua made her way over, she passed a guy in boots and knee-length shorts sunbathing on a flimsy chaise longue. He looked comfortable. If Mallory truly hadn't wanted to take responsibility that first day for a problem no one else cared about and assign

Niua to her cabin, she could have sent her to sleep out here. Interesting.

Without speaking, Niua rested her elbows on the guardrail a companionable distance away from Daphne, and they both gazed out at the waves, scanning for telltale signs of whales. No spouting or spy-hopping friends at the moment, but plenty of seabirds, which made sense considering there was a small island visible in the distance, little more than an atoll—a ring of coral breaching the surface above a submarine volcano—which would be perfect for nesting. In fact, atolls dotted the whole region, the only sign that steep mountains lurked below.

Daphne wasn't much of a talker, it seemed.

"So," Niua tried. "Hudson tells me you're trained in whale watching."

"Whale *observation*," Daphne corrected. "Whale watching is for tourists."

"Of course."

"And whales aren't the only marine mammals out here."

They certainly weren't. Even if her list didn't include mermaids. Did mermaids count?

"You must know a lot about observation," Niua said.

"Yes."

"Perhaps you could teach me?"

"I don't think so. There's a great deal of scientific training involved."

Niua fondly recalled the days when sailors understood she knew far more about the sea than they did.

This was going nowhere.

While she was thinking about what to ask next, Mallory showed up and leaned beside her on the guardrail.

Niua thought Mallory'd disappeared belowdecks to work in her lab. Perhaps someone else was using the equipment? Even so, Mallory had data to analyze. Reports to write. Colleagues to consult. She didn't have time to laze around up here with her.

But perhaps Mallory felt the same pull of gravity that Niua did, drawing them together like the moon orbiting the earth.

Had Mallory missed her? Wanted to see her? Wanted to be near her, even though they'd been apart for less than a few hours?

Niua had.

"Any update on the dredge?" Mallory asked.

"They're still trying," Niua said.

"They must be losing hope if they put you to work, Daphne," Mallory said.

They didn't need to check for marine mammals unless they planned to use the air guns, and they wouldn't use the air guns if the ship was stuck, so...yes, it was possible someone in charge thought the dredge situation was hopeless.

Daphne lowered her binoculars. "Nothing's been decided yet."

"Good." Mallory sighed. "I guess they do look like they're still working at it." She clomped away farther aft where she'd have a better view of the guys working on the winch one deck below, and peered over the edge.

Niua was tempted to follow her—with Mallory in sight, that gravitational pull was strong—but she decided to stay put, at least for a little bit. She didn't want to become Mallory's annoying shadow.

Soon Mallory headed back in her direction.

"Look, there's a ship out there." Niua extended her arm and pointed at the horizon to distract Daphne so she could have Mallory to herself for a moment. "I haven't seen another ship in ages."

"Whales are a bit harder to spot than ships." Daphne aimed her binoculars in the direction she indicated.

Mallory reached Niua and leaned on the rail again right next to her. Niua bumped their hips and their shoulders together.

"*Liquid Asset*," Daphne said. "What kind of a name is that?"

Mallory perked up at that. She followed Daphne's gaze and grasped the guardrail. "That's its name? You can see it?"

Daphne grunted. "You'd think a name like that would be on a rich guy's yacht, but it looks more like a fishing trawler."

"Or a research vessel." Mallory pulled a pair of miniature binoculars out of one of her many pockets and trained them on the distant ship. "Do you think it's that billionaire explorer who found the wreck of the *Philomena*? I watched a documentary about him. His ship was called the *Liquid Asset*."

"Could be more than one ship with the same name," Daphne said.

"I'm sure there is, but considering the type of vessel..." Mallory adjusted the focusing wheel on her binoculars. "I'll bet it's him. I was drooling over all the high-tech equipment he has."

"What kind of equipment?" Niua asked.

Mallory might well have been thinking *How much do you know about scientific equipment?* and *Is there a reason it matters to you?* and *Now are you going to admit you're a spy?* But all she said was, "Everything. He has everything. And what does he use it for? To hunt for pirate treasure."

Pirate treasure? Niua jolted, all of her senses immediately on alert.

"Why not?" Daphne said. "Pieces of eight. Gold doubloons. Every child's dream."

Mallory made a disgusted noise. "If they want gold and silver, it would be cheaper to mine it themselves. On land. Straight from the rock. Plus it would be better for the environment—and that's not something I've ever said about mining."

"That takes the fun out it," Daphne said. "You need a sense of adventure."

Mallory made a face.

She might have one, Niua almost said. Inviting her way into a near-stranger's mouth after accusing her of being up to no good wasn't on par with commissioning a treasure-hunting expedition, but they both involved a certain willingness to take risks.

Mallory leaned farther forward on the guardrail like that might help her see better. "You know what would be fun for me? If they donated their equipment to us and let us do something useful with it."

"Did the documentary say what he's looking for now? Specifically?" Niua asked.

"Another wreck," Mallory said. "Have you heard of Lennart the Pirate? Swept women off their feet and seduced them into helping him terrorize the seas four hundred years ago?"

"*Two* hundred years ago?" Niua said faintly.

"Yeah, maybe," Mallory said. "History's not my thing."

"Women weren't allowed on pirate ships," Daphne said.

"History doesn't always record the whole story," Mallory said. "Maybe Lennart bucked the trend. He wasn't exactly known for following the rules."

"That man who's searching," Niua said. "The treasure hunter. He hasn't located the wreck?"

"It's not that easy to find these things," Mallory said.

Understatement. Niua struggled not to burst into hysterical laughter and reveal how freaked out she was.

"If it's even here," Daphne said.

"Supposedly the ship sank in this general vicinity. Near the Ammonite Islands," Mallory said. "I guess you know they're west of here." This comment seemed to be directed at Niua, a pointed reminder of how bothered she'd been when she'd discovered that Niua was aware of where they were on the map, when everyone else aboard treated their navigational position as common knowledge. "Someone found a logbook. Or was it a letter? Anyway, they looked out their window and saw a ship go down. One of the pirates washed ashore the next day, barely alive. Someone nursed him back to health and wrote down who he was and what ship he came from." Mallory pocketed her binoculars. "Sounds kind of vague to me. It's not a red X with latitude and longitude out to five decimal places. But it's something."

Something? It was everything. Narrowing it down to a general location? Armed with that information, Niua had traveled halfway around the globe, confident she might be able to find the wreck. It would be harder for treasure hunters, since they didn't have her connection to the chalice. A lot harder. But with enough time and technology, it was possible they could find it, too.

There had always been the risk that others might beat her to Lennart's wreck, but she hadn't considered it a serious threat. Wreck-finding expeditions were prohibitively expensive, notoriously frustrating, and rarely successful. No one would fund such a venture without years of preparation and research. And why would they want to? To anyone but her, the chalice was a simple gold cup, and a simple gold cup—no matter how old it was— couldn't be worth all that trouble. No doubt there'd been gold and jewelry among the artwork and archaeological artifacts Lennart had stolen from the museum, and perhaps those items were enough to kindle a treasure hunter's imagination, but the possibility had seemed too farfetched to worry about. Anything else of value wouldn't have survived exposure to seawater. And if it was glory the treasure hunters were after? Lennart and his ship weren't as well known as, say, the *Titanic*, so locating his wreck wouldn't make anyone famous—not outside the small circle of the wreck-diving community. There were other—better—wrecks to pursue.

Despite all that, a potential rival was here.

Chances were, he hadn't found anything yet.

But what if he was anchored above Lennart's wreck at this very moment? Diving it and retrieving its treasure while she stood here uselessly?

She was going to have to find out. The goddess was counting on her.

13

The crew wasn't making any progress freeing the dredge.

Mallory and Jasvinder both wanted to take a closer look at the crescent-shaped atoll nearby, and the *Sea Monster* was too big to approach it, so they decided it was a good time to head over there by themselves in the rigid inflatable boat—a maneuverable dinghy with an outboard motor and space for up to five people and as many buckets of rock samples as they could fit at their feet.

Once they'd received permission to leave the ship—Captain Winata said they were making headway with the dredge, but it was likely to take a while—a couple of crewmembers helped them lower the boat into the water. Jasvinder took the seat at the controls without asking—because of course he did—but as long as they got where they were going, Mallory didn't care who steered.

She was already sweltering in her wetsuit. She dipped her hand over the side and splashed her face to cool off.

"How's the water?" Jasvinder asked.

"Great. Warm enough to swim in."

"Let's hope we don't have to."

They'd find out soon enough if conditions would allow them to land. If not, they'd have to anchor as close as they could and swim the rest of the way in. It would be inconvenient, but Mallory kind of hoped she'd have an excuse to test the water with more than just her hands. She'd stowed her diving mask and fins in the boat, and it would be a shame not to have the opportunity to use them.

Jasvinder started the motor and they sped through the gentle swell, creating a welcome breeze. "I'm surprised you didn't talk

Niua into joining us," he said.

What did *that* mean? Did he suspect she and Niua were such close friends that she'd bring her on a field trip she had no reason to be involved in? Her shoulders tensed. The truth was, if she'd run into Niua in their cabin when she'd stopped there to change into her wetsuit, she would have invited her along, because even though it was work, it was the kind of work she could share with her, and she enjoyed her company, and she might not have it for long. But she didn't want Jasvinder to know that. It felt too personal. So it was a good thing Niua hadn't been around and Mallory hadn't been tempted. She didn't want people to gossip about her being in a relationship. Especially when the relationship was in its fragile early stages and she was still figuring it out. Surely no one was paying that close attention to them, though. He had to mean something else.

"Why would I do that?" she said.

"She's always following you around."

"She doesn't follow me around."

Jasvinder laughed. "Yes, she does."

"She works with Courtland."

"He would have let us borrow her."

"For what?"

"There are sharks and barracudas out here, and I forgot to bring along a marine biologist to use as bait. Niua could have volunteered to be the first one to jump in the water to test whether anything attacked."

Not funny.

"Why are you looking at me like that, Mallory?"

"Sharks aren't always dangerous."

"Yeah, sure, I hear you. They're misunderstood. All I'm saying is, I'd rather skip the wildlife encounters."

The atoll loomed larger. They were already getting close. Jasvinder adjusted their heading to align with a break in the reef that looked passable.

Mallory glanced back at the *Sea Monster*. "I hope those guys recover the dredge. Captain Winata sounded optimistic, but..."

"He just wants to keep the scientists calm so we don't panic and get in the way."

"Agreed."

"He'll swear everything's fine right up until the minute he orders the winch crew to cut the dredge loose." Jasvinder let up on the throttle as they neared the reef. "I hope he's right, though. I don't want to have to wait another year to collect my data."

"You're coming back next year? You got a proposal accepted?"

Mallory's research proposal for next year had been rejected. So had lots of other people's. There was limited space aboard the *Sea Monster* and not every worthy project could be accommodated. She understood that. She couldn't completely repress a pang of jealousy, but this was the nature of the game. Jasvinder was a good scientist. He lucked out. Just as they'd both been lucky the last time around.

"Congratulations."

"Thanks."

Jasvinder steered expertly through the reef's underwater obstacle course and found a beach where they could safely land. It wasn't the white sand beach of tropical travelogues; it was coral shingle that shifted underfoot when they disembarked, big cobbles that slid out from under her and threatened to send her to her knees.

They'd come to see the rocks, but these were the wrong kind. Both she and Jasvinder were interested in volcanic rock, not this stuff. Not fossilized coral, and certainly not the plastic strewn on top of it. Plastic bottles, plastic footwear, plastic bottle caps, small bits of plastic that were like a new type of sea glass. It was everywhere, an inescapable human presence where humans had never been. One day, when Homo sapiens went extinct and some future form of intelligent life dug through the earth's geologic layers, it would be easy to identify this point in time—the Age of Humans—because they'd find a layer of plastic deposited across the entire planet. It was going to settle at the bottom of the ocean, get stuck in the ooze, and turn into rock, entombed forever.

Together, she and Jasvinder secured the boat and made their way to drier land. At the high tide line they encountered a storm-swept pile of colorful fishing buoys that looked like a ball pit for giants' children. Beyond that, it was all jungle.

"This is crap. We should go farther inland," Jasvinder said.

"We'll never be able to see any rocks under all that vegetation," Mallory said.

"We could get back in the boat and circle around the island, see if there's a volcanic outcrop. But I doubt we'll find another place to land. That reef is treacherous."

"So let's walk the shoreline. Seems like the only feasible option."

"Stay here." Not waiting for her reaction, Jasvinder ventured into the dense underbrush.

Mallory took a deep breath of air that stank of guano, held it, started the stopwatch function on her dive watch, and waited.

Two breaths, one recovery interval, and eight minutes and twenty-three seconds later, Jasvinder reemerged shaking his head. "We'd need a machete to deal with this. We'll have to walk along the shoreline."

You think?

"We can split up and go in opposite directions," he continued. "Cover as much ground as we can."

"Sounds good." If there was nothing of geologic interest and she decided to take a quick swim, there would be no one around to question her judgment.

14

Now that everyone was used to her presence on the ship and she'd learned the rhythms of the crew's activity, it wasn't hard for Niua to dive off the side unnoticed. Even without clothes.

She hit the water fast, no hesitation, and torpedoed through a school of sardines. The fish flowed around her as easily as water, parting and regrouping with uncanny synchronicity. Always together, always close, always driven by instinct to never, ever be alone.

Sardines survived attack by grouping together.

Her people had survived attack by splitting apart.

Fleeing.

Hiding.

Becoming invisible.

Claiming the secret, private victory of remaining alive.

Waiting.

Waiting for a future that never came. Waiting, even though everyone who'd hoped for that future was dead. Waiting, because waiting kept their memory alive.

It was hard being the last of her kind. Her family, her community—no one remained. But being a sardine would be unbearable. All that wide open ocean, and they spent their entire lives watching each other's fins. The ship had been claustrophobic enough, and no one had been hovering constantly beside her, above her, below her, close enough to touch.

She didn't envy those sardines.

She didn't.

No one would.

Even if it had been nice, for a while, to have company.

The *Sea Monster*'s hull floated far above her in a pool of sunlight that couldn't follow her all the way down. She spun away. Mallory would wonder where she'd disappeared to, but she couldn't allow such thoughts to distract her. The *Liquid Asset* was her focus now.

Just one last quick thing she wanted to take care of.

The dredge was easy to find. Mallory had told her there were no underwater cameras, so, with a few guiding echolocational screeches in the darkness of the deep, Niua swam straight to it. The cable was wedged in a crevice in a vertical rock face, snagged on the uneven surface. It was twisted—no doubt the result of the crew's attempts to release it—and the scoop dangled uselessly below.

They'd never untangle this on their own. They'd be cutting it soon, like any other seagoing vessel would, dumping waste overboard. Out of sight, out of mind. What was one more tangle of wire at the bottom of the sea? One more manmade death trap among the lost fishing nets and abandoned rope waiting to ensnarl innocent denizens of the deep who couldn't magic their way out?

She fought the current and grappled with the cable. She found some slack. Worked the cable back and forth through the crack in the rock. Tried to find the angle that would release it. A lobster snapped at her. She kicked her tail at the animal to scare it away. Gave the cable a hard tug. Adjusted. Tugged again.

The ship moved, pulling the cable taut and making it impossible to budge. She waited for the ship to change course, for the tension to ease, and tried again.

Mallory would be crushed if they lost the dredge and didn't have another one available to replace it. She'd get over it, though. She was not the reason Niua was delaying her own mission to wrestle with it. Yes, she couldn't get Mallory out of her head—didn't *want* to get Mallory out of her head—wouldn't ever forget her—but it was time to move on.

She braced herself against the rock for leverage, tightened her grip on the cable, and tugged again. The cable cleared one of the snags. Almost there. She walked her hands up the cable and tugged again. Tugged it free.

Finally. She retreated to a safe distance to wait for the ship to take up the slack.

Come on. The cable moved. The guys manning the winch had noticed the change in tension. *There.* She massaged her hands, stiff from gripping so hard. The cable rose, hesitantly at first, then faster. *Yes. Keep going, Courtland. You've got it.*

It was her parting gift.

15

As Niua approached the *Liquid Asset* and her questing screeches echoed back to her, it became clear that it was anchored above a shipwreck.

Could this be it? The pirate ship? The *Ioanna*?

She was still some distance away, but Mallory believed the *Liquid Asset*—if this was, in fact, the same boat she'd heard about—had all kinds of treasure-hunting equipment, and surely that would include cameras, so she had to approach cautiously. She couldn't allow herself to be seen.

No one could know she existed.

No one would.

She stopped kicking and let herself drift at the level in the water column where, without effort, she neither floated upward nor sank—neutral buoyancy. She spun in careless somersaults like an unremarkable piece of flotsam and allowed the current to carry her closer. Even the fish didn't pay her any attention as they streamed past.

Slowly, the ghostly wreck came into focus. Its prow was buried in sand, its mast broken, its hull encrusted in barnacles, clams, and algae. A whale skeleton loomed near the stern.

Inside, the cabins might still be intact. The chalice, if it had gone down with the ship, would still be here, caressed by waves and sand, singing the song of the long-ago people who created it—her people. Nine wise women of her tribe had forged the chalice out of gold and blood, entangling it with the spirits of those destined to become the next generation of memory keepers, and the next, and the next. Including Niua. She'd be able to hear the chalice's song from this distance—if it was here.

She heard nothing.

Another hope dashed.

But as long as there was even the slightest chance she was wrong—that she could have misjudged the distance and needed to be closer—she couldn't leave. Perhaps the chalice had been damaged by those who'd stolen it—by the priests, or the archaeologists, or the pirates—and the rough treatment had muffled its song. Perhaps its long separation from her and her sisters had weakened the bond and she'd have to be practically on top of it to hear it. Perhaps it *was* here, either inside the wreck or already aboard the *Liquid* Asset. She had to be certain.

Maintaining her distance, she scanned the hull, looking for the best way inside. Time should have worn plenty of holes big enough for her to slip through. There, and there, and…

Movement at the ocean's surface had her head jerking upward. Two scuba divers had jumped into the water. One of them held an unwieldy video camera with both hands. Two antennae protruded from the instrument. Lights beamed from the ends, piercing and unnatural.

Niua beat a hasty retreat. She'd have to wait.

This was worrisome, though. There were treasure hunters aboard up there who were likely to be searching specifically for the *Ioanna*. If they were sending divers down, they must suspect this shipwreck could be it. And she didn't know how long they'd been here. They could have been here for weeks and already have a hold full of loot. She had to be absolutely sure they hadn't found the chalice.

The divers didn't descend very far. Not many people dived the old way anymore, by holding their breath—the way pearl divers, sponge divers, and spearfishermen did—the way she herself had dived for food as a young woman, before the invaders had come and changed everything. These divers, like almost everyone in these modern times, had cylindrical tanks on their backs and hoses in their mouths. Because they carried their own air source instead of simply filling their lungs with a single breath, they needed to descend in stages to give their bodies time to adjust. The ocean allowed land-dwellers to dare breach her realm to a certain depth and no farther, and only with the utmost respect.

So while the divers waited, stuck at their present depth, counting down on their dive watches, she'd pay a visit to their friends. She didn't completely understand how their cameras worked, but she knew they weren't all-seeing. They had to be angled in the right direction, and they didn't work in swirling sediment, which impeded visibility. That meant she could swim along the bottom, kick up a storm of sediment, and move behind them to avoid detection. No one would capture her. Or kill her. Or whatever heinous thing people did these days to creatures like her.

She'd scope out the *Liquid Asset* and ask the nearest male whether he'd discovered an ancient gold cup and command him to give it to her. It would be quick. Easy. In, out, done. It would be nothing—*nothing*—like the fiasco aboard the *Sea Monster*.

If the chalice wasn't aboard, she'd return below to monitor the divers. If they found her prize, she'd snatch it out of their hands, wrest it away from them, and trust that no one would believe their tale of being attacked by a mermaid. Eventually, whether they found anything or not, they'd have to return to the surface. At that point, if she was still empty-handed, she'd take a quick tour inside the wreck to confirm it wasn't the correct one, and she'd have one more location eliminated. Only an infinite number more to go.

Her plan in place, she descended to the seafloor and swiftly detoured out of the divers' sightlines. She assessed her surroundings, decided she was safe, and, with a flick of her tail, shot to the surface. She pressed her palms to the hull of the *Liquid Asset* and took a breath of fresh air.

The ladder positioned for the divers to climb aboard was a convenient touch, as was the man who met her at the top to help her onto the deck—especially when he pinned his gaze politely on her face rather than her nudity, allowing her spell to take hold right away. There were times when being in a rush and forgetting minor details like decent clothing turned out to be advantageous.

"No...gear?" he said in a daze. The spell deepened until his jaw fell slack. It wasn't a flattering look. "Makes sense."

She held unwavering eye contact as she wrung seawater out of her hair and settled it around her shoulders. No one else was near. "I've been looking for a man who knows his way around a compass."

"You found me."

"And you are?"

"Uh...I'm...uh..." He frowned and tried again. "I'm...uh...Thad."

She nodded approvingly and flashed him a cold, practiced smile. "Tell me, Thad, have you any guesses what ship that is below us?"

"I'm hoping it's the...uh...the Ioanna."

"Really." Niua kept her smile carefully in place.

"It's a famous pirate ship. Have you heard of it?"

"I certainly have. How thrilling." He'd expect enthusiasm, and she didn't even have to fake it. She sent Mallory a mental flash of gratitude for knowing what this crew was after and for passing the information on to her. "Have you found any treasure? Any gold?" She didn't hear the chalice, but if he said no, that would confirm it.

"Nah. Not yet."

She could have kissed him. If she were the type who did that sort of thing. Which she wasn't. "That's too bad." She suspected she didn't sound all that disappointed. "But you are searching for treasure?"

"We are." He waved his hands around in excitement, recovering his energy as his mind adjusted to the initial impact of her magic. "We've been searching the area for months. Found three wrecks so far, closer to the islands, and none of them panned out. But I have a good feeling about this one. This could be the one. Gold, silver, gems...artifacts, too. Those could help us identify the ship. That's the hardest part to prove."

"You mean the items Lennart the Pirate stole from the Atlantic Museum of Art and Antiquities."

"You really do know the story. You should join our crew." Thad's expression clouded. "Wait. You're already part of the crew. You must be. Because you're here. How else would you be here."

Niua waited patiently for him to flounder around in his thoughts and decide her presence aboard his boat made sense. She'd planned to leave quickly, and he'd already told her all she needed to know, but things were going so well, she was tempted to prolong her stay. The *Liquid Asset*'s crew could potentially be far more useful to her than the *Sea Monster*'s had been. Thad was searching this area specifically for the wreck of the *Ioanna*. She was almost certain he hadn't found it, but he could have other data that would be useful—even if only to help her know where not to look.

"I need you to show me where your charts are kept. And any other locations where you believe the *Ioanna* might be, if the wreck below us isn't it. And all the information you have that led you to believe you'd find it here."

"I'll walk you there. Follow me."

Thank you, you wonderful, helpful man. You delightful, malleable...

A couple of splashes off the starboard side snapped her out of her train of thought. The divers had returned to the surface.

Her new friend remembered he had a job to do on deck, and Niua hid behind him, matching his steps as he hurried to the divers' ladder. He looked over the side, and she peered around his shoulder to prepare to make eye contact with the threat. One of the divers was preoccupied with his gear and didn't look up. The other diver was too busy throwing disbelieving gestures at his companion to notice there was a stranger aboard. She couldn't see through their masks well enough to get a clear view of their eyes, so she ducked her head behind Thad's bulk in tactical retreat.

"You're back? Already?" Thad said. "What happened?" A diver could die if he surfaced too quickly, so Thad was obviously worried there'd been some emergency.

The first diver spit out his breathing tube. "We didn't descend to the wreck."

"What? Why not?"

"Saw a mermaid."

No. No, no, no. Pain shot through Niua's feet. Her calves cramped. She clung to Thad's shoulders for balance. She was afraid if she didn't, she'd forget how to stand.

"You sure it wasn't a freaky fish?" Thad scoffed.

"I tried to get it on video, but it was too fast. Too far away. But it sure looked like a mermaid to me."

"I wanted to stay and wait for it to come back," said the second diver, "but Bentley wussed out."

Niua began to creep steadily backward and put some distance between her and Thad, careful not to appear panicky. Since running had backfired the last time.

The one named Bentley turned his back on the other diver and swam toward Thad and the ladder. "Shut up, Arturo. I draw the line at sharks and mermaids."

"Sharks have teeth," Arturo said. "What weapons do mermaids have?"

"I don't want to find out," Bentley said. "All I know is, if you don't respect Mother Nature, she will kick your butt."

"So you both saw it?" Thad said.

"No," Arturo said.

Bentley reached the ladder. "Just because I'm the only one who saw it doesn't mean it wasn't there."

Thad laughed. "Don't mention it to the environmental wackos. They'll want to investigate."

"What do you mean?" Bentley said.

"Pollution, man. Chemicals in the water. Mutant fish."

"It was no fish."

"Mutant dolphin?"

Bentley stepped onto the deck and stomped out of the way to remove his air tank. "I know what I saw."

"Do you?" Nitrogen narcosis, that's what Thad was implying. The divers' blood chemistry could have caused them to hallucinate.

"We weren't down there long, and we weren't deep. There's no way I was impaired." Bentley shook the water out of his short hair like a dog. "No. Way."

"Then go back and capture the thing. Claim a finder's fee. Sell it for the advancement of science."

"What am I now? An angler catching giant blue marlin for the prize money? That's not my skill set and we don't have the equipment, so give me a break."

"Uh-huh."

Bentley carried his tank to the spot where they stored them. He'd pushed his mask off his face. Niua had almost made it across the deck, but now she was in his direct line of sight. His gaze landed inconveniently on her naked chest. And stayed there. "Hey, who's she?" he asked Thad.

"Your mermaid," Thad said.

Niua started shaking. He *was* joking, right? Anxiously, she swept her hair across her breasts and touched her chest, her neck, her face, trying to draw Bentley's attention upward so she could make eye contact.

His gaze drifted lower.

"I'm never going to live this down, am I?" Bentley grumbled.

"Nope," Thad said cheerfully.

Niua really did like Thad. Aside from his horrific—and predictable—suggestion to capture her, he had a knack for saying exactly the right thing. She almost felt bad about the killer headache he'd have tomorrow.

"But seriously," Bentley said. "Who—"

"Does that guy need help?" Niua interrupted, pointing urgently at Arturo as he started up the ladder.

It was enough to distract him for only a moment, but a moment was all she needed to dive off the far side of the boat. As she hit the water, she got slapped in the face by a mess of sargassum. It caught in her hair, but she didn't slow down until she reached the wreck. The men couldn't—wouldn't—follow her at this speed.

She slipped through the remains of the ship she was now quite sure was not the *Ioanna*. She weaved in and out of dark compartments, around disintegrating beams, and past human skulls partially buried in silt. She strained to hear the chalice above the sound of her pounding heart, reached for it with her soul, and was met by silence at every turn.

The chalice wasn't here.

She swam away and didn't look back.

16

$\mathcal{M}$allory was alone. With Jasvinder occupied on the other side of the island, she retrieved her diving mask and fins from the boat and chose a spot to wade into the clear, turquoise water. Seabirds called noisily over the sound of the surf dragging and tumbling the shingle. She watched carefully for any indications of strong currents—she didn't want to be swept out to sea—then ventured out.

The water felt good. Not too cold at all. She explored the reef for a while, kicking lazily near the surface, marveling at the idea that she could well be the first person to swim in this ecosystem, the only human being to witness its colorful coral, clownfish hiding among anemones, schools of trevally and butterflyfish, and dozens of other species she wanted to learn the names of.

She continued to stay alert for currents, but conditions felt safe, so she continued farther out. It was a calculated risk—perhaps a dangerous one—but she ducked under, going deeper, chasing the ocean's peace.

The ocean was so calm beneath the surface, so different than the chop at the interface of wind and waves, so foreign to the rolling and pitching and swaying of a ship. Nowhere else in her life did she feel this alive. Nowhere else did she find the solace her soul yearned for. She'd certainly never found it where her parents expected her to—in the guidance of tarot cards and tea leaves and their beloved spiritual guru. The ocean was so much more compelling than any of those.

When she reached the reef's steep outer walls—the sharp drop-off where the bottom disappeared—she surfaced. Checked her position relative to shore. Took several fortifying breaths to prime her lungs. Inhaled one last time. Submerged. Kicked hard and followed the wall downward.

Thirty seconds to descend and another thirty to return left plenty of time to look around.

Many people could hold their breath for one minute. Mallory had trained herself to hold her breath for two minutes, then three, then four, then more. At first, the pressure in her lungs and throat had hit almost immediately, screaming at her to breathe. It wasn't like that anymore. She'd learned to slow her heart rate, find inner stillness, and not panic. Panicking was what got people in trouble. Panic made the heart speed up and deplete the lungs' limited stores of oxygen. If, instead, she believed she was safe, she had plenty of time. She could calmly let go and become suspended in the space between breaths, lost in time, unmoored from the boundaries that labeled *this* one moment and *this* a different moment. She had only to retain enough sanity to trust her dive watch—and remember to pay attention to it.

It was a risk, to dive alone.

Even non-divers knew you were supposed to have a dive buddy. But in reality? Not everyone did. The thing about rules was that they were designed for those who weren't experienced enough to be the ones who made the rules: Children. Amateurs. Intermediate-level employees. The rules kept them safe because there were gaps in their knowledge. When you were an expert, you understood the reasoning behind why those rules were established and when they could safely be broken. You understood that a less experienced buddy could be more of a liability than a safety measure. You understood that if something were to go wrong, even a strong diver might not be able to save you. *She* hadn't been able to save Samar...

Or you might be deluding yourself, pretending that being experienced meant you couldn't also be stupid. That *she* couldn't be stupid.

Either way, Mallory couldn't handle the thought of burdening anyone else with that responsibility. If something went wrong, she didn't want to have anyone to blame but herself.

The ocean's depths called to her. The stillness. The comfort. The deep blue dark where the emotional strain of existence dissolved and she was free.

She wanted to dissolve, but a niggle of worry held her back. She couldn't relax. She felt like she was being watched. But who could be watching? An open-mouthed moray eel? An octopus? Maybe it was nerves. Which she refused to have.

And then she saw it.

A shark.

She tensed. Tensing was bad. Tensing wasted oxygen.

She reminded herself sharks didn't always attack. This one wasn't necessarily eyeing her as dinner.

The shark had a lot of teeth. The sharp points didn't much look like the tooth she wore as a necklace. These were all lined up. And attached to a shark. Who was moving. Toward her. And very, very close.

Mallory kicked toward the surface.

The shark snapped at her. Part of the rugged plastic fin on her right foot tore off.

She was not calm.

She kicked harder. She needed to surface. Now.

Her peripheral vision faded, a black tunnel closing in. If the tunnel closed completely, she'd pass out. Then sink. At which point, if the shark backed off and didn't shred her, she'd have a small window of time during which her unconscious body could be dragged to the surface and survive. That was the reason freedivers weren't supposed to dive alone. Losing consciousness didn't have to mean drowning if a buddy was there to rescue you.

Too bad no one was going to do that.

She wasn't going to reach the surface in time.

She would have liked at least once to have dived at night and looked up through the blackness and seen the stars refracted through the water. She was sure it would have been beautiful.

As darkness closed in on her, a pair of strong arms wrapped around her waist from behind. Breasts squashed against her shoulder blades.

Mallory thrashed in surprise, instinctively fighting the person off.

Samar didn't fight when you dived down to catch her, her brain whispered. Samar had gone still before Mallory had even known she needed rescuing.

With that memory, rationality regained control. She forced herself to stop lashing out, stop resisting, because this wasn't an attack, this was someone trying to help her. Another diver? But she'd been alone. There were no scuba diver's air bubbles in the water. And that body behind her was definitely not Jasvinder's. It didn't matter. They were moving toward the sunlight. There was a chance she wasn't going to drown after all.

Her rescuer's legs kicked and brushed against Mallory's. Only one leg, really. It didn't feel right. She didn't feel knees or feet, but something flexible and boneless. Maybe it wasn't her rescuer bumping into her, but something else? A fish? An eel? The shark? With her last dregs of consciousness and a pinprick of visual field, Mallory looked down.

It wasn't a leg. It was a tail. A seal's tail. No, bigger. A dolphin's tail? Something else. It was about the same length as her own legs, and its seal-like skin glinted with flashes of silver, as if evolution had gotten confused and given a seal a few fish scales, then gotten carried away and added magnificent whale-like—mermaid-like—flukes.

It wasn't a mermaid. There was another explanation for this, and it was that Mallory's oxygen-deprived brain was in the midst of a well-documented physiological response to the increased pressure the body experienced underwater. It was called narcosis. The rapture of the deep. Vision narrowed; sea anemones danced to a drumbeat; rocks were laid out in mystical diagrams that pointed the way to new discoveries; mermaids with gold serpents coiled around their arms carried drowning divers to safety.

Narcosis. Had to be. It was always a danger.

The mermaid's tail slammed down hard and propelled them toward the surface.

Mallory's vision went dark.

17

Mallory was drifting in a strange dreamscape of saltwater and seaweed and mermaids. It was a good dream, where she belonged with someone who cared about her. She wanted to stay in the dream.

But her consciousness was being dragged back into her body. Small rocks pressed against her spine, and she felt the caress of air—not water—on her face.

She wasn't dead.

She'd been rescued. A mermaid had wrapped her arms around her and...

That couldn't be right. A *person* had wrapped her arms around her and hauled her to the surface.

And then...and then she didn't remember what happened, but she must have been dragged onto the beach, and now someone was gently stroking her forehead, smoothing her hair away from her closed eyes, waiting for her to wake. Mallory sighed with pleasure. No one touched her like this. With caring. With tenderness. Women always wanted her to be the strong one, and most of the time, she wanted that, too. She liked being competent and unbreakable. But right now, it felt good to be taken care of, after the shark and the tail and the burning need to breathe.

And the bracelet.

Her breath quickened. She knew that bracelet. That gold spiral coil. Not a pair of twisting serpents, but familiar hard metal. That had been Niua's bracelet. Niua's forearms.

But not Niua's legs.

No. Niua was on the ship. Mallory had looked for her before she left for the atoll and hadn't found her, but she'd been aboard somewhere. She wasn't here on the beach with her.

So who *was* here, touching her? And why couldn't she figure out how to move her eyelids?

Words formed in her mind, but her mouth wouldn't move. Neither would her throat, which would have squeezed shut to prevent water from entering her lungs, even while unconscious—a reflex she apparently wasn't ready to fully let go of. She tried again, and a groan escaped.

The touch stopped. Pulled away. Feet scrabbled on the shingle.

No! Mallory couldn't speak, couldn't see, couldn't move.

There was a splash, distinct from the crashing surf.

She coughed, and the force of it drove her eyes open. The bright light of the sun stung. She blinked and coughed and rolled to her side. Red drops hit the sand. Blood.

She was alive, though. That was good.

And alone.

Niua hadn't expected to see Mallory ever again. She wouldn't have, either, if her echolocational scan of the route ahead hadn't revealed that Mallory was in the water. Mallory wasn't supposed to be underwater; she was supposed to be safely aboard the *Sea Monster*. Niua had sped toward her. The danger had been as bad as she'd feared.

She didn't understand why Mallory had been swimming alone, but now that Niua was farther from shore, an inflatable boat of the type used for shore excursions was visible on the beach, as well as a man who paced impatiently nearby, no doubt wondering where Mallory was. That was a relief, because it meant Mallory would be able to get back to where she belonged.

Niua watched, confident she was an indistinguishable dot bobbing in the waves.

She was sure Mallory had not seen who'd rescued her. Niua had approached from behind, and Mallory had never turned to see her face. She'd been too scared by the shark or too close to losing consciousness to concern herself with her rescuer's identity.

It was better this way. She didn't want Mallory to know.

At least...that was what she *should* want. But if she was completely honest with herself, she did want her to know. She yearned to know that Mallory liked *her*—the real her.

But that would never happen.

Over the years, there'd been women who promised to love her forever, but when they were faced with the reality of a creature who looked the way they expected her to look for only one month in a generation, they changed their minds. Whatever the prevailing culture, whatever civilization rose to power, any woman who learned the truth found her body repulsive, her very existence unacceptable. The invaders had won. Her society had been wiped out. No one remembered her goddess, and chances were, no one ever would. No one would ever look at Niua and see the human being she'd once been. Mallory would be no different.

Niua waited until Mallory rose and began to make her way back to her little boat. Then Niua ducked beneath the waves, slapped the water harder than necessary, and dived into the deep, off to continue her search.

Not everyone was meant to find love.

Not everyone had a choice.

Who had rescued her?

Mallory didn't see any boats, the atoll was uninhabited, and she was much too far from the *Sea Monster* for anyone to have swum from there.

Too far...

Just as they'd been too far from shore—four days' sail from shore—the first time Niua was noticed aboard their ship.

No. It couldn't have been Niua out there, saving her from that shark. That was ridiculous. Niua wasn't... She wasn't a mermaid.

Mallory stared at the water, wondering how she was going to explain her mauled fin to Jasvinder, and whether she'd feel guilty if she dropped it on the mounds of plastic already on the beach to avoid having to talk about it. He'd notice if she returned with only one fin, though, so it really wouldn't solve anything.

The sea rippled with a gentle swell. Did she see a…? It was hard to tell from a distance, but she thought she could make out the outline of a person's head before it disappeared. A moment later, a dolphin's tail kicked in the air.

Mallory watched the sea for a long time.

Whatever she thought she'd seen, it was gone.

18

C limbing up the hull of the *Sea Monster* at night under a waning moon was less fun than riding the CTD bottles the way Niua had boarded the first time, but the CTD wasn't in use, and besides, this route was less likely to be noticed. She'd had too many close calls lately.

She clambered over the guardrail and scanned the open deck for complications. At the opposite end, a silhouetted man paid her no notice. She didn't see anyone else in the shadows. Good. She removed a stray clump of sargassum from her hair, adjusted her brand new sargassum-colored dress, and went inside in search of Mallory. Not because she couldn't stay away, but to make sure Mallory'd survived and to ascertain whether she'd seen who—or what—had rescued her.

That's what she was telling herself, anyway. But even she could see it for what it was: an excuse.

What was she going to do if Mallory *had* recognized her before she blacked out? Hope she'd forgotten? Hope she didn't imprison her in a laboratory? Hope was not a plan of action. Her feelings for Mallory were not a reason to put herself at risk.

Nothing could kill her underwater in mermaid form, but out of the water, in human form, she was unprotected. If she was trapped, and the moon turned full, and she wasn't safely back under the waves…well, that was why she was the only mermaid left.

And yet here she was, because it had been so long since she'd felt like this about anyone that it was clouding her ability to think.

She shouldn't have come back.

She finger-combed her hair and continued down the passageway. Her heart pounded, and she told herself it was excitement, not fear.

There was a certain cognitive dissonance involved in making small talk in the mess at Captain Winata's birthday party, standing under whimsical paper cutouts of disproportionately buxom mermaids in scallop-shell bikinis dangling overhead, and smiling while a group of geophysicists played guitars, when a few hours earlier, Mallory had been about to die.

Physically, she was fine. A scuba diver in a similar situation might not have been, but diving on a single breath meant a swift ascent hadn't harmed her. Mentally, though, she was shaken. It was difficult to offer encouraging *uh-huh*s at the appropriate pauses in conversation when all she could see was those strong arms wrapped around her waist and that incongruous tail. Had someone—some*thing*—really been in the water with her? Or had she saved herself and only imagined she'd had help?

She took a cupcake that had more frosting than cake from the buffet and drifted over to where Niua was having some kind of confrontation with Courtland.

"Where were you?" Courtland looked like it wasn't the first time he'd asked.

"You didn't need me," Niua said, gesturing dismissively with a cupcake of her own, that distinctive gold spiral coil wrapped around her wrist like always.

Had Niua missed her shift? Mallory thought about lying semiconscious on that beach, wondering who was watching over her, puzzling over the dreamy touch on her forehead. The fact that Courtland hadn't been able to find Niua around the same time didn't mean she'd been at the atoll. She couldn't have been. She'd been somewhere on this ship, socializing or napping or charming her way into other people's business. Courtland could hardly expect a person who'd been forced into the job to be a model employee.

"You didn't know that," Courtland said.

Cupcake poised near her mouth, Niua toyed one-handedly with the neckline of her dress. It was the same clingy dress she'd worn the day they'd first met. The fabric had faded from olive brown to a splotchy yellow-brown—had it accidentally gotten bleached in the laundry?—and she must have tracked down a needle and thread, because the torn sleeve looked as good as new.

"You didn't know, because you didn't ask," Courtland said.

It was fascinating to watch her fuss with her clothing. Perplexing, too, because although it was one of her typical bullshit moves she deployed to draw attention to her body, Mallory knew what Niua looked like when she was interested, and this wasn't it. She wasn't flirting. She didn't even look like she was aware of what she was doing.

"It's true, though, isn't it?" Niua answered Courtland. "You were fine without me."

"That's not the point."

Niua licked neon green frosting off her cupcake the way she might dare him to look at a repellent infection on her tongue. "Perhaps I was ill."

Courtland was undeterred. "Then why didn't you say so?"

Mallory turned hastily away to avoid being noticed and having to join in the conversation. As she did, a paper mermaid hit her in the face. She brushed it away. It snagged in her hair. Frustrated, she ripped it apart and stalked off to the garbage bin with it, where June—the cook she'd once spilled coffee on—stood laughing at her.

"Not a mermaid fan?" June said.

Out of one conversational hazard, into another.

A mermaid may have saved my life today. Mallory wasn't going to say *that*. She didn't believe in mermaids. There had to be another explanation. She tossed the crumpled party decoration in the bin.

"They're supposed to be sexy," June said.

"Why? Because they don't wear clothes?"

"That's a start, isn't it?"

"I like to think I'm better than that." Mallory glanced over her shoulder to double-check she was far enough away that Niua wouldn't overhear. Just in case. "Besides. Not that I don't appreciate dangerous women, but...luring sailors to their deaths? Doesn't that seem...I don't know...*not* sexy?"

"That part's not important," June said with a dismissive flick of her fingers. "Their deadliness? That's a myth."

Mallory was in too weird a mental state to sense whether June was joking. "Their whole existence is a myth."

"If they don't exist," June argued, "then why does every language in the world have a word for them?"

Every language had a word for dragon, too, because ancient people found dinosaur fossils in eroding cliffs and didn't know those bones were millions of years old, so they imagined giant winged lizards flew overhead unseen and nested in mountainside caves. It proved nothing.

"Look at that face." June snickered. "You're trying to decide if I'm serious and whether you'll offend me if you explain that the existence of mermaids is scientifically impossible."

"Actually—"

"I'm messing with you."

That was a relief. Mallory had been about to say the existence of a never-before-documented new species wasn't impossible, only highly unlikely, but she was happy not to get into it.

"I imagine they *would* be deadly, though," June added, "because the worst kind of monster is the one who doesn't look like a monster, because it can fool you into trusting it. A colorless marine worm wriggling in the current? Ick. You keep your distance. Those...*things*...live down there in the dark for a reason, and that reason is that no one has to see them or think about them or display them on their fancy computer monitors and then get all excited and say 'Hey! Look at this!' to unsuspecting cooks who might happen to be walking by minding their own business." June threw up her hands in a *what-are-they-thinking?* gesture. "But a beautiful woman sunbathing topless on a rock? You let down your guard."

"Not everyone—"

"So be careful with whatever it is you're doing with our stowaway, all right?"

Mallory startled.

June nodded in Niua's direction. "You've been watching her all night."

"No, I haven't." She wasn't stalking her. She wasn't obsessing. She was simply confirming that Niua was here on the ship looking the same as she always did. She was gathering data so as not to jump to conclusions based on incomplete information. Niua would understand that. *You measure the sea's depth at Point A and at Point B and draw a lovely straight line between them, and then you're surprised when you run aground on a reef.* And if there appeared to be drips of water staining the back of her dress, well, the sea spray did often reach the open deck.

"You're *not* watching her," June said. "Right. My mistake. You're coincidentally facing in her direction everywhere she goes."

Was she being that obvious? "It hasn't been all night. She's only been here twenty minutes."

June started laughing again. And no wonder.

Despite herself, Mallory smiled. "I just proved your point, didn't I?"

19

Mallory wasn't sure how long she lay in her cabin in the dark, thoughts spinning with memories of the coral reef and the shark and the pressure in her lungs and the panic and the way her vision distorted before she blacked out and her conviction that she hadn't been alone when she regained consciousness on the beach.

Could she really have surfaced, unconscious, on her own? The principle of Occam's razor suggested that a simple explanation was more likely to be correct than a more complicated one. But which was the simpler explanation? That she'd been rescued by a mermaid? When everyone agreed mermaids didn't exist? Or that she'd imagined a mermaid while experiencing nitrogen narcosis, a well-documented danger that countless divers could attest to?

She'd broach the topic tonight when Niua returned to the cabin. She'd ask her not to laugh, because she wanted to ask her something, and it was going to sound farfetched. She'd tell her she knew Niua might need to lie, but she couldn't not ask, not when there was a chance Niua might tell her the truth and her answer might make everything make sense.

Then Niua's lips would twitch. She'd cover her mouth and try hard not to laugh. She'd shake her head and ask Mallory if she was serious and did she honestly believe there was any chance she wasn't exactly what she appeared to be? And Mallory would be a little embarrassed, but at least she'd know she hadn't been afraid to question what she believed.

She was still awake when Niua let herself in. There was a rustling of fabric that meant Niua was undressing. Mallory waited silently—anxiously—to find out what Niua would do next. She sensed her approaching, and then Niua was slipping into bed with her, finding space, because fitting two people into their narrow bunk always involved a certain amount of nudging and rolling. It was all perfectly ordinary.

Mallory felt along the bulkhead to click on the bedside light. Niua was *not* a mermaid, but Mallory wasn't going to fall asleep next to her without... She couldn't believe she was thinking this, but she needed to see.

Niua blinked in the sudden light. "You're awake." She found Mallory's hand and brought it to her lips.

June had made a good point about appearances being misleading, but Mallory didn't believe for an instant that Niua posed a threat to her. All she wanted was for Niua to hold her, and for it to be true that Niua had saved her.

If.

If Niua was more than what she seemed, she'd worry about whether Mallory had seen her underwater, wonder if Mallory suspected. Would she even be here? This ship wouldn't be a safe place for her.

If.

If she was...what Mallory thought there was a possibility she might be...then Niua was in danger, and she was going to leave.

And Mallory wouldn't stop her. She'd help her leave. Help her stay safe.

She didn't want her to leave yet. So Mallory said nothing. She didn't ask. Not yet, anyway. She hauled Niua on top of her, and smiled with all the nonthreatening, *I-didn't-see-anything* reassurance she could muster, and kissed her.

It was a full-body kiss.

Mallory gripped Niua's ass, clutching at her like she couldn't get enough. Niua hiked one knee up to her waist to crawl up her body. Mallory rubbed the back of her thigh appreciatively from her ass to the crease of her knee and all the way back up. She explored her inner thigh, her outer thigh, everywhere she could reach.

Which was good for Niua's ego, but…did Mallory always stroke her lovers' legs? Did she always trace their shape?

Had Mallory seen?

No. She couldn't have. Niua had been careful.

Although not as careful as she could have been. It would have been safer to do nothing—to not rush in, in a panic, and save her life. To not sit at her side on the beach worrying until it was clear she was all right. To not return to the ship and climb into Mallory's bed and risk another slip that would give herself away.

But it was worth it.

Because she loved her.

She wasn't going to say it, because it couldn't lead to anything. They couldn't build a life together. Their relationship would be over before it ever had a chance to begin. She'd known that from the very first moment, and perhaps that was why she'd fallen for her so quickly, because it had freed her to dive in with all she had and not worry what would come of it.

So Niua told her with her mouth and her hands and the sliding of her body on top of hers everything she couldn't bring herself to say.

I love you, she mouthed into the space between Mallory's breasts, over her heart. *I want to be with you forever*, she nuzzled into the hollow at the base of her throat. *I don't want this to end*. Kiss after kiss, touch after touch, she silently poured her emotions into her, willing them to seep into her skin. So Mallory would know, deep in her soul, everything Niua wanted to say.

I wish we could belong to each other.

Her throat clenched shut and choked on the words.

They couldn't belong to each other.

They couldn't.

Mallory rolled onto her side, taking Niua with her. She curled around her, bending her knees and fitting their legs together, front to back, wriggling into place, eliminating the space between them.

She kissed the back of Niua's neck—sweetly, confidently, possessively. She wedged her knee between Niua's legs.

"Oh." Niua clamped her thighs together reflexively, trapping Mallory there. It was easy to forget she could separate her legs and that Mallory could get inside, but it felt good having her there. She released her death grip and arched her spine, pushing backward into her, wanting her closer.

Mallory pressed up hard.

That was...ungh...good.

And not enough.

Why was Niua the only one naked here? She rolled away and flipped onto her knees, freed Mallory of her objectionable sleepwear, and straddled one thigh.

Better.

She worked her hand between Mallory's legs. Mallory sighed like she'd been waiting for her. She was beautiful on her back, flushed and quivering and briefly hers.

Niua found a rhythm that made Mallory's breath catch, and matched it with the undulation of her hips. She loved doing this, making Mallory happy, feeling Mallory's reactions echo through her own body. She could come like this. Heat coursed through her and pooled at the base of her spine. Her thighs tingled in jittery warning. A glimmer of worry flittered at the edge of awareness, but she was too lost in their connection to pay attention. She bent to find Mallory's mouth. The wildness of the ocean rose within her, raw and powerful, unstoppable, pushing to be set free. Soon she was going to lose control...

Wait.

Niua broke the kiss and panted, struggling to catch her breath, staring at Mallory with her black, fathomless eyes.

In another context, Mallory would have said the look in her eyes was fear, but Niua dived in and kissed her again, and it didn't feel like fear, it felt like she wanted this, like she meant it, like kissing her was the most important thing in the world.

Niua was molten and slick against Mallory's thigh, and that knowledge was going to make Mallory lose it faster than the steady strokes of Niua's hand.

An urgent sound rumbled in Niua's throat. She pressed hard into Mallory's ready body, deep and insistent. Mallory gasped and closed her eyes. It was perfect. Pleasure built inside her like a powerful wave, promising to take her over. She wanted it. She wanted it so much. Niua was getting off on this—grinding her hips, finding where Mallory wanted her, making Mallory writhe and buck and make noises that didn't even sound like her. Mallory clenched around Niua's fingers, too far gone to do anything but feel. She couldn't get enough of her. She wanted the wave to keep rising. She wanted the wave to break...

Above her, Niua let out a wild, choked cry. Mallory thrust upward.

It was Niua who broke first. Her legs squeezed sharply together. She slid off Mallory's body. She kicked the bed hard, just once. The mattress bounced. Their hips bumped.

The contact felt strange, her skin tough and slippery.

"What..." Mallory's eyes flew open. And she saw it.

Huge inhuman flukes fanned across the foot of the bed and draped over the edge. An indistinct line below Niua's waist marked the transition from skin to rubbery hide, glinting with patches of silver scales.

She was still inside her.

Mallory came with violent, helpless spasms, over and over and over again.

The moment Niua stopped seizing with aftershocks and she regained control, she reversed her body's transformation.

And ran.

Of course she ran. Running was the only thing she knew how to do.

20

The slam of the cabin door jarred Mallory out of her shock and into motion. She cursed and grabbed her shorts and sleepshirt from the floor and pulled them on. It cost her precious seconds, but she couldn't bring herself to run naked through the ship in pursuit, not when Niua had a head start and there was no hope of catching up.

What was she going to do if she caught her, anyway? Beg her to stay? Niua wasn't going to stay. Not this time. And this time, Mallory understood why.

She shoved on her boots and chased after her anyway.

She didn't see her in the passageway, but it wasn't hard to guess which way she'd fled: up to the trawl deck. To the ocean.

Getting there didn't take long.

The trawl deck was abandoned. It was the middle of the night, and although plenty of people were awake and working, they were all belowdecks.

Mallory rushed to the nearest guardrail and squinted into the darkness, breathing hard. The sea was black and impenetrable. The moon played peekaboo behind a mist of clouds. If there had been a splash when Niua escaped overboard, she didn't hear it.

Niua was gone.

Mallory was sure of it.

She bowed her head and tried to catch her breath.

"You didn't have to go…" Her words dwindled away into silence.

I wouldn't have hurt you, Niua. I would have kept your secret.

The weird details that Niua hadn't done a perfect job of hiding and that seemingly only Mallory noticed rearranged themselves, explained by the stunning truth.

Was it strange that she wasn't horrified by what Niua was? She was probably supposed to freak out. Or...as a scientist...be intrigued? Excited that she'd discovered a new species?

She wasn't. Niua wasn't a *thing* she'd discovered. Mallory was never going to tell anyone about her. Never write a paper about her. Never use her, never exploit her, never endanger her to advance her own career.

She'd been foolish that first day to force her away from the guardrail. If Mallory hadn't been so sure she knew best, Niua could have gotten away right from the very beginning. No one would have even noticed. Niua wouldn't now be afraid she'd placed herself and her entire species in humanity's crosshairs. Guilt roiled Mallory's stomach and threatened to make her vomit over the side of the ship.

Niua had chosen to stay, though. She could have slipped away at any time during the past five days. Why had she stayed?

So many puzzle pieces made sense now, but there were others that still didn't fit.

Mallory was scared for her. How could Niua have put herself at risk like this? What was she thinking? What was so important that she'd befriended a ship full of curious scientists when she could have stayed safely hidden underwater?

A mermaid. She couldn't believe it.

She *could* believe it.

She knew better than most people how easy it would be for a species that rarely came ashore to remain undiscovered for centuries. The sea was the best place on earth to hide: vast, hostile, and unexplored. The idea that a mermaid had made her way onto the ship was improbable, but not unthinkable. And when faced with compelling evidence, a true scientist was willing to change her mind.

As a child, Mallory had believed in supernatural beings. Of course she had. She'd been raised by parents who talked about fairies and ghosts as if they were as real as squirrels and trees. Whose guru claimed to communicate with psychically evolved extraterrestrials. Not physically, of course. On another plane. Where only the special, chosen few were spiritually advanced enough to sense them—which conveniently explained why doubters couldn't.

Eventually Mallory became disillusioned. Her mother called it teenage rebellion; Mallory called it growing up. She retained her connection to spirit, but transcendence was something she found underwater, alone.

Joining the scientific community had been a relief. She'd found a new home among people who tested their theories rather than place their faith in a single leader's infallible wisdom. Nature was the ultimate authority. Data ruled. No one argued that if a person wanted to understand why fish did what they did, it was more valuable to communicate with the creatures on the spiritual plane than to listen to experts who actually observed them.

And now…this.

A mermaid.

For real.

Who could shapeshift. That part, as far as Mallory was concerned, was magic. There was no way mankind's current level of scientific understanding could explain instantaneous shapeshifting. And she was okay with that. How often had she been frustrated watching new ideas be ridiculed or dismissed as bad science? Or unexplainable phenomena be ignored? When questioning the status quo was supposed to be a scientific ideal? It didn't have to be one or the other, either/or. She could do both: Relentlessly pursue knowledge *and* be in awe of the unknowable. Test hypotheses *and* believe in unsolvable mysteries.

Considering how many years she'd spent being angry at her parents for their weak commitment to logic, it was less embarrassing than she would have predicted to think there might be a place for magic in her life after all. It felt comforting. Because if shapeshifting mermaids were real, then Mallory's entire childhood hadn't been a lie, and her parents hadn't been stupid to believe every word their beloved guru said, because somewhere in all his self-serving garbage there'd been specks of hard, glittering truth.

21

The Ammonite Archipelago was a group of dozens of small tropical islands, most of them unnamed, untouched by humans, and too insignificant to appear on any map. Two centuries ago, on one of these islands, someone had witnessed the pirate ship *Ioanna* sink in a storm. Only one man aboard survived. He washed ashore, barely alive, and was nursed back to health by an islander who recorded the event in a diary.

But which island?

The television program Niua had seen through a houseboat's window on the other side of the world hadn't specified, but there had to be plenty of people familiar with the details, and she couldn't afford to remain at a disadvantage. Thad—the treasure hunter—was exactly the kind of problem she didn't want. He would have done his research. He would know. In theory, she could use the *Liquid Asset*'s position to narrow her search area, but there were too many islands that could have been his starting point, and each one spawned vast areas of possibility. In practice, his location didn't help all that much.

When the month was complete and the moon was once again full, Niua would return to the sea. She'd swim a search grid. She'd search until she'd covered the entire area around every one of these islands, no matter how many years or decades it took. Eventually, she'd find the wreck. But swimming a grid was slow, and she'd perpetually worry that Thad and his divers—or others like them—might beat her to the wreck and disappear with the chalice without her even knowing. She'd keep an eye on them, of course, but she couldn't do that all the time, not when she was conducting her own investigation.

Better to learn as much as she could while she was able to walk on land. That was why she'd come to the largest island in the archipelago.

The harbor smelled overwhelmingly of dead fish. It was the end of the day, and fishing boats were returning home with their catch. Fishermen bustled about, hard at work. Niua stood on a pier, wooden boards under her bare feet, and chatted up a friendly fisherman who'd happily abandoned his work to talk.

"Have you heard of the wreck of the *Ioanna*?" she asked, skipping the pleasantries.

"Oh sure. Everyone knows the *Ioanna*."

"The pirate who survived. The one who made it to shore. Which island was that?" Presumably it was one of the eight islands with a significant human presence, but who could know for certain where some hapless soul had tried to make a go of it two centuries ago?

"You're standing on it."

Was she truly so lucky that she'd found the correct island already? "In which direction does the wreck lie?"

"Some say to the south. Some say to the east. Some will say anything to a pretty tourist." The fisherman's assessing stare made her feel like she was a prize fish he wanted to measure. "You one of them treasure hunters?"

"I take it that means I'm not the first person who's come asking about the *Ioanna*."

"Not the first, no."

Not the answer she wanted to hear. She had little to be concerned about from amateurs in search of adventure, but the very idea that anyone else had their sights set on *her* wreck was unwelcome. Thad was bad enough. "What did they ask?"

"Same thing as you: Do I know where the wreck is? Can I guess where it is? What are the rumors?"

"What did you tell them?"

"Nothing."

"Is that what you're going to tell me? Nothing?"

"There's nothing to tell."

"No wrecks at all around the island?"

"Plenty. I know a guy who takes tourists out to dive a beauty out there on the reef. Tells them it's a hundred years old. Truth is, it's nothing but a fishing boat that went down twenty years ago. I know the guy it belonged to." He scratched the back of his head. "The wrecks that are really a hundred years old, they're falling apart. How would anyone know for sure which ships they were?"

"Any wrecks farther out?" The *Ioanna* was unlikely to be a tourist attraction located in the clear, shallow water close to shore. Someone would have identified it by now. Past the reef, where the ocean was much deeper, it would be hidden.

"Can't see anything farther out."

"You don't need to see the bottom with your own eyes to suspect what's down there."

Finally, he smiled. "I'll tell you what. The big wrecks? The fish love them."

She nodded like this was news to her and waited for him to say something useful.

He paused like he wanted to make sure she was paying attention. "Those are the secret fishing spots no fisherman's going to tell you about because he wants to keep them to himself."

Oh yeah?

It wasn't even a challenge. One good, hard stare and those fishermen wouldn't be able to wait to reveal their secrets to her.

And they did.

The problem was that everyone had secret fishing spots where the fish were unusually plentiful, and those locations were scattered in all directions. Many fishermen spoke of visible shipwrecks, and those, too, were everywhere. There were too many wrecks, too many islands. And—as she'd been warned—every one of those wrecks was supposed to be the *Ioanna*. The pirate was a local legend, and everyone wanted to claim him as their own. *Trust me*, they said. *The wreck is here.* Every island she visited, *that* was the island where the pirate washed ashore. The folks on the other islands were embellishing, trying to steal the credit, but this island, this was it.

It was hopeless. The moon was waning, the nights counting down, and after days of fruitless conversation, Niua was no closer to finding the Ioanna than she'd been when she arrived.

She had hoped the answers would be here, waiting for her in the islanders' minds. She hadn't expected to need to consult a neutral party. A scientist, perhaps. Someone like the researcher mentioned in the television program she'd seen years ago. He would know where the diarist had lived. If he still worked at the same museum, she could track him down. In Australia. Near Mallory's university. Where Mallory would be returning in a matter of days.

A detour was tempting.

And risky, because although she did have time to change tack, she knew if she traveled to Australia she'd want to look for Mallory, and that might end badly.

Mallory might see her as a scientific discovery and try to capture her. She might be scared of her. She might be repulsed by her. She might hate her. She might want her, but think she shouldn't, and hate herself for it, and blame Niua.

Over the years, Niua had seen all those reactions and more. It would hurt to face them again.

Especially when part of her insisted Mallory wasn't like that—that when Mallory had gripped the backs of her bare thighs like she was trying to convince herself Niua did not have a tail, it was because she'd already known, and it hadn't disgusted her.

Hope was a tricky thing. It led to bad decisions. And to good ones.

An ocean breeze whipped at the hem of Niua's dress.

She could live without knowing how Mallory felt.

She just wasn't sure she wanted to.

22

Mallory had never been the type of person who needed someone in her bed to help her fall asleep, but this expedition had been full of surprises, and for the fifth night in a row, she found herself pacing the trawl deck in the dark, watching the moon wane from three-quarters full to half full to crescent-shaped when she'd rather be asleep.

Niua was out there, somewhere, and if anything happened to her, Mallory would never know.

Her stomach hurt. She didn't think it was seasickness.

In the morning, the *Sea Monster* would return to port. Maybe she'd be able to sleep once she was home, where the stars were less breathtaking and the waves less close. She had samples to make room for in her lab, colleagues to catch up with, a conference presentation to prepare for, and more.

She usually would have been excited about that.

She usually didn't get involved with women who made her unable to focus on her job.

Over the years, in her endless failed attempts at dating, she'd tried to make it work with lots of different types of women, hoping to find the right personality that would click with her own, at times even treating it like an experiment, never ruling anyone out based on superficial qualities. But a mermaid? Really? That was taking things too far.

Except they *had* clicked. She *had*—finally—found someone she could truly fall for.

And in the end, it didn't matter, because Niua had left, too, the same as all her other exes.

Not because Niua didn't like her, though. She was sure Niua had liked her.

And Mallory…Mallory had loved being with her. Loved her.

She had, hadn't she.

She wished she'd told her. Instead, she'd reminded herself she didn't know Niua well enough—which, to be fair, turned out to be true—and held back on expressing her feelings out of fear that anyone with as many lust-addled fans as Niua would never want anything serious with someone as boring and uncharming as Mallory.

Her stomach flopped like a fish that did not want to be hauled out of the water. Her throat closed, choking on air. Once again, she'd failed at a relationship.

Now all she could do was stare out at the whitecaps on the black water and blink up at more stars than she'd ever seen from land and watch for a shooting star to wish on, when she didn't believe in wishes or shooting stars or the possibility that Niua would ever return.

Returning to Australia made the emptiness worse.

Mallory should really have been in the lab getting work done and getting back into her routine, but instead, she was perched on the same granite boulder she'd been sitting on for hours on a remote stretch of shoreline where few people ventured and only seals sunbathed.

She should have been thinking about her research, not losing herself in the sound of the ocean, not watching the tide change, not solving her Rubik's Cube. The cube was the one she'd fished out of the sea and given to Niua. It had never turned smoothly, but it hadn't mattered to Niua that rotating the pieces required a bit of effort, because she'd turned the sides slowly, trying to see the patterns in the colors. For fast solving, a stiff cube like this one ought to be thrown out and replaced with a new one fresh out of the box, but Mallory had no intention of replacing it. She felt like a teenager, touching an object Niua had touched and imagining they were touching each other, hand over hand, together on a ghostly plane where the past and the present overlapped.

She gave the cube another frustrated twist. The activity was pointless, merely something to keep herself busy. She had plenty of more productive tasks she could—and should—be working on. She couldn't just sit here all day. She could, for example, work on the travel arrangements for her upcoming trip to a volcanology conference where she'd be speaking about her research. She'd been looking forward to the event for an entire year, but now the airline had informed her that her flight to Jakarta had been canceled and her reservation transferred to another flight that landed too late for her to present her paper. She needed to fix that. Which, fine. She often didn't have the energy to deal with the annoying details of daily life. But conferences where she got to share her research hadn't ever fallen into that category.

She stopped twisting the cube and dropped it in her lap only two-thirds of the way solved. She flattened her palms behind her and leaned her weight on her arms. The waves were hypnotic. Over a week had passed since she'd last seen Niua. The moon had waned from a crescent to a bare sliver on the horizon visible just before dawn that vanished into the sunrise. This morning, there had been no moon at all.

A pang of longing hit her so hard she swayed. It seemed absurd for a person who'd never fully found her sea legs on the deck of a ship to also fail to regain her land legs when she returned to solid ground. Fitting, though. A mermaid had rocked her off balance, and nothing would ever be the same.

23

The Ammonite Islands were scenic and remote and attracted a fair number of yachts accustomed to traveling great distances. Many of them were small, leisurely vessels that would take weeks to arrive anywhere.

This one, though. This yacht looked showy and sleek and expensive. It looked fast.

Its passengers must have thought it odd for a woman to leap off a sailboat and swim over to greet them, and even odder for her to inquire from the water about their average cruising speed, but the man who owned the yacht was too powerful for anyone to question why he invited her aboard. Perth had not been his intended destination, but when Niua explained she needed a quick way to reach the continent, he was happy to oblige.

They always were.

24

I t was rare to encounter other people in the secluded cove where Mallory spent her mornings walking up and down the beach, her only company a group of seals who didn't flee when she approached.

She liked it that way. She liked being alone, tracking the ripples of seaweed and broken shells left behind by the receding tide. She didn't want to be around other people. Even when they didn't try to make polite conversation, even when they pretended she wasn't there, their mere presence grated on her skin. She was always like this after living in close quarters for weeks at sea—like she'd used up some essential nutrient and needed time to replenish it—but this time it was worse.

It was irrational, but anyone who crossed her path? She was angry they weren't Niua. *Not you*, her body bristled when she spotted a stranger. *Not you*, her soul protested when she spoke with a colleague. *Not you*, her mind screamed at the world. *You're not the one I want.*

Here, she could relax. And maybe accept that she'd lost her.

She stood at the edge of the tide, where the sea kissed the sand, and let the water reach her bare toes.

What had Niua been doing on the *Sea Monster*, anyway? She'd obviously been looking for something in the acoustical scans. But what? What information was she searching for, and what was so important about it that she'd risked being discovered? Mallory would've helped her if she'd asked. Not at first. Not when Niua was driving her to distraction trying to make sense of her contradictions. But knowing what she did now, if Niua came back and asked, things would be different.

"I hope you're all right," she said into the wind. Helplessly. Hopelessly. Ridiculously, but there was no one around to hear, and saying it out loud soothed some of her anguish. She felt for the shark's tooth she wore around her neck and remembered how Niua had stood too close and fingered the shark's tooth and it felt like she was touching her.

"I wouldn't have told anyone. I never will."

She rolled up the cuffs of her trousers and stepped deeper into the water. It was cold when it flowed over her ankles—she was much farther from the equator than she'd been on that fateful dive with the shark.

She'd never thanked Niua for saving her life.

"I wouldn't have let anyone hurt you. I would have kept you safe."

She closed her eyes. The wind caressed her face. Her cheeks felt wet.

"I love you."

The roar of the waves continued unchanged.

The sea should care. The sea was heartless. It was never going to notice her feelings.

"Niua!" Now she was shouting, digging the heels of her hands into her eyes, making a fool of herself, feeling stupid, but she couldn't seem to stop. "I'm sorry I scared you. I'm sorry I didn't make you feel safe enough to be yourself."

The seals barked like a disapproving audience.

"I wish I'd told you I loved you." The words kept spilling out. "I don't know if that would have made a difference, but I wish I'd told you. I wish I'd realized sooner. I wish I'd been braver."

She pushed her fingers through her hair and watched her feet sink deeper into the sand.

"The seals are wild animals, you know," called a female voice from down the shore, out of sight. "It's best to keep your distance." She sounded exactly like Niua.

Mallory's heart leapt. Was it her? Could it be her? Could it really? Or was it someone else with a similar voice?

Where was she? Behind the rocks? In the water? Mallory whipped around, urgently scanning her surroundings.

There she was: bobbing in the waves, dipping beneath the surface and reappearing much closer, dark hair plastered to her head. Niua.

Mallory ached to run to her and hold her in her arms and tell her how much she'd missed her, but she was rooted to the ground. The last time she'd seen her, Niua had run from her without a word, clearly afraid. There was a good chance she didn't want Mallory to get too close. Otherwise, wouldn't Niua be racing onto the beach with her arms outstretched?

Niua pushed her hair out of her face. "It's safer that way."

Mallory was trembling. "Are we still talking about seals?"

"Do you really love me?"

She'd heard that? Mallory cringed with embarrassment, but she pushed past it because she wasn't going to let Niua think she posed a danger to her, not now, not ever again. "Yes," she said, trying to convey with that single word all the passion and certainty in her heart. Her feelings were not in question. "I do. I love you. I love you so much. I can't believe you're here."

Niua disappeared underwater again. She wasn't going to leave, was she? Had Mallory said the wrong thing? Had she scared her off?

No. She didn't believe that. There was no plausible reason Niua would have coincidentally swum to this insignificant cove that happened to be near where Mallory lived. If Niua was here, it was because she'd come looking for her. She wouldn't have come if she didn't feel something for her.

She was *here*.

Mallory unfroze and ran into the spray. A line of waves barreled into her and knocked her down. She swam then, arm over arm, barefoot but fully clothed, determined not to let Niua slip away.

And then Niua was swimming toward her, too, and meeting her

halfway, and Mallory was kissing her, and Niua was kissing her back, curling her tail possessively around Mallory's thighs and undulating to keep their heads above water.

"I found you," Niua said, sounding awed and happy, like it was a miracle.

It kind of was. Mallory grinned wider than she thought possible. She didn't know how Niua had done it, but she'd gotten here. Because of her.

"I thought I'd never see you again," Mallory said.

Their hands were all over each other. Niua's strong tail swished steadily, keeping them afloat. It was the strangest feeling, but Mallory loved it, because it meant Niua wasn't hiding what she was. She wasn't trying to pretend anymore.

"How did you get here so fast? It would take me years to swim that far. Did you find another boat?"

"I met a lovely Russian man who was impressed by my command of his language. His yacht was quite pleasant."

Mallory laughed. "You're such a user."

"He insisted he would enjoy the journey with me."

"And then you abandoned the poor guy."

"He'll get over it. All I care about is you."

Niua kissed her again, harder, until Mallory's head was spinning. They sank under the waves, still kissing.

Mallory had to let go then. Surface. Splutter. Breathe.

Niua caught her, turned so her back was to Mallory's chest, and positioned Mallory's arms around her bare waist. She overlapped their forearms and locked her fingers around Mallory's wrists. "Don't let go."

Mallory guessed what was coming and drew in a breath.

They dived.

It was like how Mallory imagined riding a dolphin would be, but better, because the sea creature she was clinging to and trusting with her life was the woman whose mind and soul she trusted with her heart. With a flick of Niua's tail, they streaked through the water. They rode up waves, plunged down the other side, came up for air, whooped with laughter. It was exhilarating. Terrifying. Wild. Perfect.

Eventually, Niua swam them back toward shore. When they reached shallower water, Niua curled her tail around Mallory's legs and rolled her into a playful spin. As their rotation slowed, Niua pulled her knees up and curled in on herself, shivered in Mallory's arms, and sank them both toward the bottom. Was Niua cramping? Was she all right? Mallory took over and dragged her to an abrupt rise in the sand where Niua had clearly been headed and where Mallory could stand with her head above water. She straightened, hugging Niua to her chest and pulling her up. Breathed. Niua regained control of herself and stood with her. On legs. Like nothing out of the ordinary had happened.

"I love you, too," Niua said, tangling their fingers together. "Take me home with you?"

25

Mallory had felt guilty about her repeated absences from the lab since she'd returned from her expedition on the *Sea Monster*, but now that she had a new reason for missing work, she had absolutely no regrets. Not when Niua was leading her through her own house toward her bedroom with a determined glint in her eye.

Outside the bedroom door, Mallory hesitated. One of the two seaweed-colored sundresses Niua had left behind on the ship—identical to the one she'd conjured on the beach ten minutes ago in front of Mallory's stunned, wide-eyed gaze—lay balled up under her pillow. Unless Mallory was trying to impress a date, she never made her bed or straightened the pillows or paid any attention at all to how the bed looked, so there was a chance the dress was not, in fact, under a pillow, but somewhere visible. Was she going to ask Niua to wait while she hid the evidence? No. She could handle a little embarrassment. She didn't need to hide that she'd missed her.

Niua nudged her through the door. There was no sign of the dress.

"Good navigation skills," Mallory said.

"Stick with me, and you'll never be lost."

Niua eagerly tossed her new dress and Mallory's salt-encrusted clothes in a damp pile on the floor, lowered Mallory onto the bed, and flopped on top of her like it was the only place she wanted to be. The briny, exciting scent of the sea—and of the woman she loved—was everywhere. Mallory could hardly believe how lucky she was.

Niua propped herself up on her arms, elbows on either side of Mallory's head. A droplet of water fell from her hair onto Mallory's shoulder. "On the ship. When I shifted? I'm sorry I startled you."

"You don't have to apologize."

"The shift... It's not something I can control. When I let go, my body takes over. I didn't mean to—"

"Didn't mean to what? Be with me? Be honest about who you are?" Unexpected hurt burned in Mallory's chest. "Do not apologize for that. I'm *glad* you lost control. That's kind of the point, isn't it? When we—"

"But you weren't expecting my body to—"

"I'm glad I know," Mallory said firmly. "I want to know you. This is part of who you are. Yes, I was surprised, because it's not the sort of thing anyone would imagine was a possibility, but it's not like I didn't know there was something about you I didn't understand. I love you, okay?"

"It truly doesn't bother you? What I am?"

"There is nothing about you that would make me not love you."

Niua's eyes shimmered with emotion. "I feel the same way about you."

"You're safe with me. Like I said on the beach. You heard that, right?"

"That's why I'm here."

"Okay. Good."

Niua bowed her head. Her hair fell across her face and brushed Mallory's shoulder. "I want you to know it's not your fault I ran off. I would have done it no matter what. It was instinct."

"Okay." She hated what it meant that Niua needed that reflex. "Why'd you come back then?"

"Hope."

"Thank you for trusting me." Mallory rubbed her cheek against Niua's forearm, the closest part of her she could reach. "Does that mean you're here to stay?" Where did mermaids live, anyway, when they were on land? They couldn't exactly rent an apartment without money or identification. "Will you live with me?"

"Let's talk about that later."

Mallory wasn't going to like this, was she. "Promise me we're really going to talk about it."

"I promise."

"Whatever's going on in your head, whatever it is, I can handle it. Please don't run off again without giving me a chance."

Niua held her gaze steadily. She didn't say *You can trust me, too*, but she did not look like she was planning her escape.

"Please," Mallory said.

"You're very sweet."

No one had ever called Mallory sweet. "Most people would call this being too intense."

"You've been intense since the day I met you," Niua said fondly. "I like intense. Especially on you."

"Yeah?" Mallory was sure the smile she gave her was shy and happy and not like her at all.

"I'm not here only for your body. You must know that."

Mallory flushed. Niua was rather intense herself.

Niua swept her hair in a pattern across Mallory's chest. "I know this isn't a good enough answer, but I'll...try."

Mallory shivered. She pressed the soles of her feet into Niua's calves. "I love you."

Niua wiggled on top of her, looking pleased, and traced a path down Mallory's body with her mouth. Apparently she was done speaking.

She slid her hands behind Mallory's waist, then downward to grip her ass. Slowly, deliberately, she buried her face in the crease at the top of Mallory's thigh. She wasn't even doing anything—just breathing—but it felt overwhelming. When Niua looked up, still holding her tight, her gaze was full of helpless, desperate need.

None of the women Mallory dated had ever looked at her quite like that.

Of course they hadn't. Mallory only dated women who were self-confident and more than capable of taking care of themselves. They had enough experience to have lived through a few failed relationships and had learned to never fully commit. They could be passionate, but not vulnerable.

Niua had more reason than any of them to put up a wall. The world was not a safe place for her. And yet she was willing to let her feelings show.

Her need.

Her want.

Her desire.

As if she had no sense of self-preservation.

Mallory hadn't thought she'd like it. She'd thought this sort of thing would make her uncomfortable. She had no interest in damsels in distress.

But Niua wasn't helpless. She wasn't clingy. She didn't need Mallory—or anyone—for anything.

The sight of Niua panting and dazed and trembling for her didn't make Mallory want to push her away. It made her want her more. It made her desperate for her. She wanted to make her whimper and hyperventilate and shudder and more...and more...and *more*...until Niua couldn't hold on anymore and lost control—*really* lost control—and shifted.

She was never going to get enough of her.

Mallory blinked awake. Niua's leg had her pinned to the mattress; her face was tucked under Mallory's shoulder. Mallory rumbled happily and stretched her arms overhead. Niua adjusted so there was absolutely no space between them and nuzzled her breast like she belonged there.

"Love you," Mallory said. "Love waking up with you."

Niua wiggled suggestively.

"Yeah?" Mallory said.

The idea of sleepy lovemaking early in the morning had always held a certain allure, but she'd never been with anyone who was into it.

She'd tried. But Poppy had been all business in the morning, racing to get to the office or to her scheduled weekend activities. Ashanti had been grumpy in the morning, so Mallory had learned to keep her distance. Valencia had looked at Mallory like she was a pervert, and after that, it was hard to suggest it to anyone else.

Mallory did understand wanting to get to work on time, or not being in the mood, or not liking it. She did. And she'd accepted it. There were lots of things she'd never have and that she was okay with never having. Life was full of small disappointments that weren't worth dwelling on.

And yet…

She slid a hand softly up the back of Niua's neck and into her hair, hoping she wouldn't move away. Niua made an encouraging murmur and cupped Mallory's breast. Tears stung Mallory's eyes with salt.

Niua wanted this.

Wanted her.

Mallory hid her face in her biceps to blot her reaction. "Feels good," she mumbled.

Niua stroked up and down her side, finding the underside of her arm and working her way to her forearm, exploring Mallory's body as if she wanted to remind herself of everywhere she'd been and ingrain Mallory's secrets in her memory. Niua settled on top of her, their breasts jostling until they nestled into the place where they fit. Mallory squirmed underneath her, chasing the feeling of skin against skin.

"You all right, *mein Schatz*?" Niua asked.

Mallory blinked rapidly to clear her vision. "What's that one mean?" She rocked her hips under Niua's weight. She wanted to feel, not think. "It means *hippopotamus*, doesn't it?"

Niua smiled and rocked with her, matching her rhythm. "Not quite."

"*Iguana*?"

"No."

"I'm going to hate it, aren't I?"

"You won't." Niua kissed her temple, an oddly sweet

counterpoint to their nudity and the steady, insistent rocking of their hips.

"Hmm." She imagined Niua was capable of seducing women in a dozen different languages—a hundred different languages, because anything was possible with her—key phrases at the ready. Maybe it was naïve of her to hope Niua would use those endearments only on her and on no one else, ever again, for as long as Mallory lived, but that was what she wanted. "You like that I can't tell if you're making stuff up."

"It means *my treasure*."

"Oh." The tenderness in Niua's voice caught at her heart, and something deep inside her clenched hard. "If you say it like *that*, like you want to get me naked, you can call me an iguana anytime."

"*Mein Schatz.*" Niua kissed Mallory's nose. "You're already naked." She kissed her again. "And I wouldn't lie to you."

"About this," Mallory corrected.

Niua held her gaze for so long that Mallory started to wonder if Niua actually had lied outright while they were on the ship, or only avoided telling her the truth. Niua sighed. "I wouldn't lie about this." Her lips brushed Mallory's cheek. "Not about this, my treasure." She held Mallory's shoulders to steady herself and placed a tiny kiss on the corner of her mouth. "Pirate's treasure." Their lips ghosted together. "Hidden underwater, where no one can see how beautiful you are."

Beautiful? No. She wasn't beautiful. She didn't want to be. She didn't want the kind of attention that beautiful women were forced to tolerate. She was fine with being gruff and competent, and with being left alone.

"I, however," Niua continued, her words forming shapes against Mallory's lips, "am not afraid of the sea."

Mallory tried for a deeper kiss, but Niua eluded her, because apparently Niua was under the delusion that talking was what they should be doing right now. Mallory whimpered a complaint. She could reach her hair, though, so she sank her fingers into it and stroked the back of her head.

Niua's eyes drifted shut. Her neck arched. Her spine undulated lazily in a ripple of desire. It hardly seemed real that Mallory—who'd tried so hard to make her girlfriends happy and had never truly managed to succeed—could elicit such pure adoration.

Mallory raised her head to try again to chase Niua's mouth. This time Niua gave her what she wanted, opening to her like she regretted having pulled away. They kissed like they needed to do it to survive. They dived in again and again and again until Mallory was the one who broke it off—and Niua slid down her body, her hands hot on Mallory's thighs, to finish it.

"I found you," Niua breathed, her voice catching, "and someday everyone else is going to wonder how they could have been so blind."

The next time Mallory woke, mid-morning sun shone through the bedroom curtains. The sheets were on the floor. Niua sat beside her, knees together folded mermaid-style, combing tangles out of her hair and meeting her gaze with a contented smile.

How did this comfortable togetherness fit with Niua's comment that someday other people would appreciate Mallory's supposed treasure-like qualities? What had she meant? That they'd admire her from afar, because they'd missed their chance? Or that someone else would be in Mallory's bed, because Niua would be gone?

"You're awake." Niua straddled Mallory's hips and lowered her weight onto her thighs.

Mallory drew gentle circles and hearts with her thumbs on Niua's legs. It was time to get answers. "You can't live with me because you can't live on land all the time. That's what you're going to tell me, isn't it? It would make sense. Your natural habitat is the ocean."

Niua let out a long, sad sigh, and Mallory knew she was right.

But why? There had to be some way they could make it work. Niua had stayed aboard the *Sea Monster* for days, so it wasn't impossible for her to leave the water. "You promised we'd talk about it."

"I did."

"You could live with me part-time. Return to the sea and come visit me when you can."

Niua's gaze shifted down to her legs. "There's something I need to do today." She was already changing the subject. Great. "I could do it myself, but it would be easier if you helped me."

"I'll help with anything you need." What she *wanted* to help her with was to find a way she could stay. But she doubted that was what this was about.

"Will you take me to the marine archaeology museum?"

Mallory blinked. She didn't know what she'd expected, but it wasn't this. "The one here in town?"

"Yes."

"Of course."

"There's an employee there I need to speak with. Could you help me locate his office?"

"Should be easy. I'll call and make an appointment."

"Oh." Niua looked thoughtful. "I suppose it would help to know in advance if he's going to be in his office."

Mallory pursed her lips. "So your plan was to surprise him and hope he wouldn't shut the door in your face?"

"Yes?"

It made a weird sort of sense. There wasn't much use for phones and appointments underwater, after all. "I'll call."

"But if he says no, don't press. I don't want him to warn his gatekeepers."

"His gatekeepers? You mean his administrative assistant?"

"Right."

"I don't think you need to worry about that. You'll walk in, and you'll do that thing where you smile at him and he helps you get away with murder. He won't know what hit him."

"He's not the one I'm worried about." Niua hesitated. "I thought you didn't like it when I flirted."

"I understand now why you do it."

"You do?"

"It's your way of getting what you need. On land, you're powerless, and flirting is the only tool you have to convince people to help you." It wasn't Niua's fault that society didn't allow her better options. "If it doesn't bother you, and it means you're able to take of yourself..."

Niua looked bemused.

"*Does* it bother you? Because I'd be happy to talk to him for you if you want me to. If it's not a social call. If he has information you need?"

"I don't know if that's a good idea."

"Why not? I know how to navigate this world. I have a car and a phone and resources." Niua had fit in inconspicuously—mostly inconspicuously—aboard the *Sea Monster*, but she was bound to run into problems sooner or later. "I'm sure you could do this by yourself, but you don't have to. Whatever it is. We can do it together. We can be a team."

Niua joined their hands and interlaced their fingers. "We're already a team."

"We could be more," Mallory argued. "I'm not asking you to tell me anything you don't want to tell me, but let me help. I want to."

Niua kissed Mallory's knuckles one by one. She didn't speak until she'd made it all the way across. "All right."

26

Good sex had a way of making Niua stupid, making her say things she had no intention of revealing. It was annoying. There was no need for her to tell anyone what she was searching for or why. Mallory would help her even if Niua kept her in the dark. But that felt like taking advantage of her. She wanted Mallory know.

Know her secrets.

Know her.

"I don't want to mislead you," Niua told her. "I love you, but I will have to leave. I can't stay."

Mallory sucked in an unhappy breath. "Are you sure?" Her face contorted. "No. Sorry. Of course you're sure."

Niua hated this. She didn't want to do this to her. "I'd stay if I could. If regular dips in saltwater were an option, things would be different."

"What if I lived down by the marina? Or on a houseboat. A sailboat?"

Niua gazed down at herself sitting on Mallory's thighs. She barely recognized the shape of her own body. "It's not like that."

"Then what is it like?"

How often had Niua wished for a person to love who didn't disappear the moment she revealed her true nature? Let alone one who tried this hard to stay with her? At some point she'd given up hoping, because it seemed impossible.

It seemed she hadn't given up entirely.

She wanted her to know.

"Once upon a time—"

"Seriously?"

"Yes, my little iguana, seriously."

"Sorry," Mallory said. "I'm listening."

"Long ago, my people lived on the coast of the North Sea in harmony with the earth and the sea and the sky. Our goddess protected us. In return, nine chosen women protected and preserved her wisdom. I was one of the nine. A memory keeper."

The day she joined that sisterhood, she gazed down into their sacred chalice, saw a flash of reflected sunlight, felt the dirt beneath her toes, joined her voice with the others' in song. She saw the future, and it was beautiful.

It was short-lived.

"When invaders first arrived, we were a small tribe. We hid in the swamp. The tidal marsh. The forest. We knew the terrain. They didn't. We survived. They moved on."

"A tribe," Mallory said flatly. "Do you know how long it's been since Europe has been inhabited by tribes?"

"I have some idea, yes."

Mallory grimaced. She was either doing the math in her head or trying to decide whether Niua was lying. "You're saying you're immortal."

"No."

"But you've been alive since…when?"

"I don't age. But I can be killed."

"And you were born with a genetic variant that allows you to become…"

"No." Niua squeezed her knees around Mallory's thighs. She swallowed. She didn't have to do this. She could stop. But she hoped some good would come of this. "I'll explain."

"Okay." Mallory's expression softened, reacting to Niua's distress, shifting from incredulity to compassion.

"The next time the invaders returned, telling tales about primitive, evil beings who lurked in the swamp, we weren't so fortunate."

Mallory stroked her bare legs soothingly, anchoring her in the present, reminding her she was safe.

"We ran from the slaughter, some of us into the forest, some of us into the sea. The nine of us—my sisters, the memory keepers—chose the sea. Arrows rained down around us, piercing the water. We dived underwater, away from the attack. The arrows kept coming. We dived deeper. If we stayed down too long, we'd drown. If we surfaced for air, we'd be hit. I stayed down."

Mallory's hands shook, but she continued to stroke her, trying to calm her, and perhaps trying to calm herself.

"I was holding our sacred chalice. The memory keepers' chalice. I'd grabbed it during our escape. I should have dropped it so I could swim unencumbered, but I was too terrified to think of it. And then, amidst the slap of arrows, the goddess spoke. *Swim*, she said. *Kick*. I swam for as long as I could, distancing myself from shore, the other memory keepers alongside me. *Surface*, she said. I did. I gasped for air. I was alive. I turned and looked back, and I was so far away that the attackers' arrows could no longer reach me. I could scarcely believe I'd been able to swim so far on a single breath. I looked for my family, my friends, everyone I knew..."

Mallory held Niua's hands and pressed their clasped fists to her chest. To her heart. Mallory's love was an almost palpable feeling, expanding and embracing her.

Niua had hoped her heart could no longer break, but that was the trouble with being unable to forget. Remembering everything meant events never scabbed over into old, healed wounds. They were always there, ready to bleed again.

"The ocean should have been teeming with people, but there was no one. Blood stained the waves."

Niua closed her eyes, swept up in the past. "*Retreat*, the goddess said. *Hide. Survive.*"

She squeezed her eyes shut more tightly. "We had no way to fight back."

"You survived," Mallory said. "You did what you had to."

Had she had a choice?

"My sisters and I circled together. One of them ducked under and dived. She kicked into the air, and I saw what she'd become. What the nine of us had become. What I'd become."

"You were turned into mermaids?"

Niua nodded. Opened her eyes. Pulled herself out of the worst of the memories. "Our tribe was wiped out. But we were the goddess's memory keepers. She changed us so we could live." Her voice cracked. Went hoarse. "Hide. And live."

Mallory's hands were warm and steady on hers.

"Together, we retreated to the safety of the sea. The goddess hid herself in the deep ocean where no one would ever find her. She suspended her breath. She suspended time. The world continued to move forward, but the goddess herself was no longer swept up in the stream of human lifetimes. There are some who whisper there are others like her who sleep until the day they will be reawakened, but she is not asleep. She is…"

Silent.

Waiting.

Being.

Still.

"The mermaids' purpose is to remember her—and to remember the civilization that honored her—because if she is forgotten, she cannot return. We keep her memory alive, and we wait, in the ocean, where nothing can harm us." Niua swallowed. Not *we*; not *us*. The slip was unsettling. It meant some part of her was incapable, even after all this time, of understanding that her sisters were gone. "I wait. I am the only one who remains. The only one who remembers."

"The others were killed? How could that happen if nothing can harm you?" It took Mallory only an instant to understand. "Oh. In the ocean. That's what you said: nothing can harm you in the ocean. They were killed on land."

"Yes."

Mallory's hands clenched protectively around hers. "Then why are you here? Why risk it?"

"She did not want us to retreat forever. She wanted us to be able to breathe among people, live in modern society, and retain our humanity, so when she returns, we…I…will be ready to return as well." It was the goddess's nature to spiral and cycle, so… "Once every eighteen years, I am able to live on land for one month, immerse myself in the culture, spend time with people, and imagine the future."

"While taking your life into your hands," Mallory bit out.

"So you see why I can't stay."

Mallory was silent. Like she was thinking hard and didn't like the conclusions she was reaching. "You knew from the beginning this would be temporary."

"You'll find someone else."

"You think I'd be happy, settling for someone else?"

"It doesn't have to be settling."

"It will be if it's not you."

They'd both gotten in way too deep. "I can't stay." If she had the chalice, this would be a different argument, but she didn't, so there was no use thinking about it. "It would be eighteen years before I could see you again."

"In this body, you mean. You could still—" Mallory looked bewildered. Vulnerable. "Isn't there any way we can make this work? I mean, I get that you thought this would be a short-term thing, and I didn't expect it to turn out like this, either, but we have something now. We're good together. Can't we try?" She worried her bottom lip. "Do you not want to be with me?"

"It's not that."

"It sounds to me like it is."

"*Wanting* isn't the issue."

The look Mallory gave her made her feel like a wayward square on the Rubik's Cube—squares Mallory always managed to get where she wanted. "It's been almost three weeks since we met. When did your month start? How long does that leave you? How long does that leave *us*? Because I'm going to convince you to change your mind."

"I have until the full moon."

"You're kidding me." Mallory let out a harsh, disbelieving laugh. "The moon? The moon cycle stuff is real?"

"The moon governs the tides. Why should it not be possible that it would affect someone like me?"

Mallory gripped Niua's waist and hauled herself up to sitting, a worry line between her eyebrows. "What phase of the moon are we in now?"

It never ceased to surprise Niua that people no longer kept track of the moon, a habit that had been so central to human existence for so long. "It's a waxing crescent moon."

Mallory looked blank. "I should have learned basic astronomy. What does that mean? How many days does that leave you?"

"Ten."

Mallory sagged and visibly relaxed.

"But there's a lot I need to do in those ten days."

"Like visit the guy at the museum."

"Right. I need…" It was hard to continue, but this was why Niua had told her about her past, wasn't it? There was no reason to stop now. Choking, she said, "I need his help to find the chalice."

"You lost it?"

Niua bristled. "I didn't lose it. It was stolen."

The worry line reappeared. "And this man knows where it is."

"He can point me in the right direction." Niua buried her face in Mallory's chest. She hoped she hadn't made a mistake in trusting her with more of her secrets.

"I'm going to help you, remember? We're going to get it back."

Niua nodded, burrowing into the space between Mallory's breasts. "Help me forget? Just for a little while."

"For as long as you'll let me," Mallory murmured. She lowered Niua onto her back and crawled up her body, balancing on her forearms to take some of her weight off her.

That wouldn't do. Niua wanted her weight. She squirmed beneath her and spread her legs wider. She curled one leg around Mallory's waist, pressed her heel into the small of her back, and reeled her in.

"It took you a couple days to relearn to use those amazing legs of yours, but you're pretty good with them now."

"No one on the ship, including you, thought there was anything out of the ordinary about my stumbling."

"Yes, my love, you were very convincing."

Mallory's tongue found Niua's hard nipple. Niua jolted. Mallory licked. Swirled. Sucked. Lingered. Held her nipple between her lips until it got even harder. It was just this side of unbearable.

Niua was sure she looked wanton. Writhing. Whining. Begging Mallory to give her what she needed. To fill her with good memories. To remind her of words like *transcendent* and *perfect* and *I wish I could belong with you*. To reach inside her and touch her soul.

Her hips surged up to meet her. The small of her back tingled and arched.

Her climax caught her like an ocean wave that didn't know its own strength, tumbling and flipping her until she lost all sense of up or down, leaving her no choice but to surrender to its power.

She shifted.

Mallory ran a reverent hand over Niua's flank and down the length of her tail.

Niua hadn't believed anyone would ever do that. It had seemed unthinkable. Impossible.

She didn't shift back, just to see how that felt, to not immediately react like her tail was something to be embarrassed about. She felt off-balance, but it was no match for the afterglow. She stretched languidly and fit herself into the curve of Mallory's body.

"This chalice," Mallory said. "Does it have anything to do with why you were aboard our ship?"

"You're still bothered by that?"

"I'm very, very happy you were there." Mallory kissed her neck like she wanted to prove her point, sweetly and deliberately, still worshipfully caressing her tail. "But yes, unanswered questions do bother me. You know how I am."

And yet Mallory had not asked why she wanted the chalice. Apparently, its sacredness was enough of a reason.

If they were going together to the museum, Mallory would find out soon enough what Niua had been up to on the ship, so… "I was hoping your sonar scans might help me locate it."

"It's in the ocean?"

Niua nodded.

Mallory let loose a long, satisfied sigh of understanding. "So many things make sense now."

It felt good to see her happy, but a vague sense of unease lingered. How many more secrets was she going to be tempted to reveal?

27

D r. Adam Hollingshead was a talker.

Niua leaned forward in her chair—one of several the man kept for visitors in his office at the Museum of Indo-Pacific Marine Archaeology and Maritime Anthropology. She propped her elbows on her thighs, rested her chin on her hands, and kept her eyes wide open and interested—all while trying to ignore Mallory's fidgeting in the chair beside her. "I understand you know where the pirate ship *Ioanna* sank."

"That wreck certainly does attract a lot of attention," he said.

"Does it?"

"There's no logical reason for it."

"There isn't?"

"Even before that Bronze Age cup was stolen, when it was on display at the Atlantic Museum in France, before it ended up at the bottom of the sea, it was of limited archaeological value. We presume to know its age because we can compare it to other artifacts, but where did it come from? Was it part of a collection held centuries ago in the church where it was unearthed? Or was it buried in a deeper, older soil layer that the church was built on top of? Given the imprecise excavation techniques in use at the time..." He shook his head in professional despair. "But no one cares. Because no one can resist pirate treasure. It captures the public imagination."

"Where is the wreck?" Niua asked in an attempt to steer the conversation away from this tangent. She couldn't bear the thought of her chalice in anyone else's hands. It had already been taken from her once.

"I should have never agreed to be interviewed for that television program. They completely sensationalized my research."

"You're saying you don't know where it is?"

"I'm not saying that at all." He proceeded to explain about the sparsely inhabited islands, the home renovation, the rotting walls, the diary, the yellowing pages, the humid environment that meant it was a miracle the pages hadn't disintegrated long ago. Then he moved on to the disappointing news coverage, the reclusive homeowner who raged at him when the media got wind of the discovery, and his failure to locate the wreck himself.

"So you could give me the coordinates of the area where the *Ioanna* was last seen?"

He turned to his computer and tapped at a keyboard that made mechanical clicking noises. "I'll look that up for you right now."

Mallory coughed. Niua risked a glance in her direction and found her unsuccessfully trying to hide a smile. She was glad Mallory'd developed a sense of humor about Niua's skill at convincing men to come to her assistance. Niua batted her eyelashes exaggeratedly at her. Mallory's cough turned into wheezing.

"The Ammonite Islands are quite remote," Adam said, obliviously fixated on his screen. "Your devices won't have any connectivity out there. I'll need to print the map out for you on paper."

A machine across the room hummed and spit out an oversize sheet of paper. Adam retrieved it and made room for it on his desk. It was an aerial photograph overlaid by topographic contour lines. "Here's where the house is located." He marked a star in blue pen on one of the islands and scrawled the address and its coordinates at the top of the sheet. "Here's how far I calculated the observer could have seen from this location, based on the telescopes of the day." He sketched a curve radiating outward from the house into the ocean. "There are multiple potential lines of sight, and the diary didn't specify a direction, but the fact that a survivor reached the island, given the prevailing currents, makes me believe the sinking must have occurred in this area." He marked off a smaller area and copied several sets of coordinates from his screen onto the edges of the paper.

Niua thanked him politely. She neatly folded the map and tucked it into her pocket.

As they left the museum, Mallory said, "I'm canceling my conference trip."

"What conference?" Niua said.

"I'm supposed to give a presentation, but this is more important. I'll buy us plane tickets to the islands and we'll leave as soon as possible."

28

Mallory didn't doubt that Niua would have found a way to get to the Ammonite Islands, locate the specific island indicated on Adam Hollingshead's map, rent the equipment she needed, and charter a fishing boat on her own, but Niua did seem appreciative of Mallory's logistical skills. When Niua disappeared for several hours and returned with a handful of gold coins to cover their costs, Mallory didn't comment on the way the coins were cemented together in a clump—or the barnacles—and she quietly stopped worrying about her bank account.

As Adam had warned, the island where the diary was found was sparsely inhabited. The closest place to stay overnight she could book on short notice was a guesthouse located several islands away across the archipelago. Their only disagreement involved the charter boat, which Mallory found on yet another, more populous island, and which Niua vetoed. *No female captains*, she said, and she didn't even look embarrassed by her sexist attitude. Mallory argued there was nothing wrong with the boat and they didn't have time to waste being particular, but Niua didn't budge. Mallory found another boat.

Their new captain was surprised they didn't want to fish. Niua explained they were scientists, and that was enough to end any further questioning. He didn't so much as grumble when she asked him to turn off the engine a dozen times a day so she could lower a hydrophone into the sea in silence and listen. The hydrophone was not an instrument on any treasure hunter's supply list, but she needed it, she told Mallory in private, because the chalice sang. At a frequency, Mallory was disappointed to learn, only Niua could hear. Niua didn't know what the chalice's range was—sound traveled farther in water than in air, and when the thing had been in her care, it had been hidden in a sea cave, wedged in rock beyond the reach of the tide—but she was eager to listen for it. Mallory was in charge of sonar. She hadn't operated sonar equipment since her graduate school days, but she hadn't forgotten how. Mallory recommended other equipment and suggested hiring help if they could afford it, but Niua insisted they had all they needed.

The days passed quickly. They sailed search grid patterns, discussed where on the map they should try next, and enjoyed each other's company, always aware that their few remaining days were counting down.

"I love this technology," Niua said, watching the sonar image on the screen with Mallory, her arm around Mallory's waist, her head on Mallory's shoulder the way others might watch a movie. "The information is so detailed." They were both impatient that they hadn't found anything yet, but Niua seemed to be able to find moments of joy in the process regardless of their results. "Did you know that centuries before any sailor ever laid eyes on it, Antarctica appeared on world maps?"

"How'd that happen? Did mermaids whisper the planet's secrets to the cartographers?"

"Certainly not." Niua's huff made it clear what she thought of that idea. "It was a lucky guess. There was this one seafaring captain…"

"Isn't there always?" Mallory said fondly.

Niua laughed. "Nice guy, really. I asked him why the shoreline of the southern continent was drawn incorrectly on his map— profoundly incorrectly, I might add—and he explained it. Said it wasn't wrong, it was hypothetical. They drew it on their maps because they believed that if the earth was a sphere, it was only logical for there to be a southern landmass to balance the weight of the northern hemisphere's landmass."

"The weight." Was Niua serious? Of course she was serious. She'd been there. "Because if one pole had extra mountain ranges that made it heavier than the other one, the planet would fall out of the sky?"

"Exactly."

"Unbelievable." It was staggering how far science had come in the past few hundred years. And yet Niua's tribe had been able to do what modern science couldn't even begin to comprehend: they could shapeshift. "This is why no one believes our ancestors could have been right about the existence of mermaids. It doesn't occur to us that they actually saw you."

"Very few did. Being noticed has always been dangerous for us, so we try to avoid it. But people back then didn't demand proof the way you do. They trusted the word of their priests."

"Why'd the priests think you were real?" Mallory hugged her close, grateful those years were behind them. "No, wait. I know why. They were like any other guru. They couldn't admit there was anything they didn't know. Right? There couldn't be a mermaid hypothesis, only mermaid fact."

"They used us to scare their congregants." Niua pressed her face into Mallory's shoulder. "But they scared us, too. It's easier to stay hidden when you're a myth."

"We'll keep it that way," Mallory promised.

Niua nuzzled her neck. They fit so perfectly, like they belonged in each other's arms. There had to be a way they could stay together.

"I've been thinking…" Niua disentangled herself and pulled the by-now well-worn map out of her pocket. She unfolded the paper, smoothed it against her thigh, and pressed her index finger to the spot where the diary was found. "I know Adam examined the site and talked with the homeowner and saw the position of the windows himself, but if we had more time, I think we'd have started here at the house ourselves instead of trusting this map."

"You don't trust it?"

"These search parameters are based on modern information.

We've been assuming it's accurate, and I believe it is accurate, but it's accurate for today. The *Ioanna* sank almost two hundred years ago. The tides and currents may have changed since then."

She was right. The earth was always changing. Mallory was used to thinking of large-scale processes that occurred slowly, but on the local level, change could be swift. Two hundred years was more than enough time for this stretch of ocean to be not quite the same as it once was.

Niua circled her finger around the mark. "I want to visit the island where the eyewitness was. See if we can find clues to how the area may have changed."

It would be a gamble. What new information could they hope to find in a day or two? Research took time, and time was running out.

"It's going to be the full moon in two days," Mallory said.

"I know. But I want to try."

29

It was dark when they waved goodnight to their captain and returned to the guesthouse. As soon as they were in their room and had closed the door behind them, they removed their boots and collapsed on the bed. Niua lay facedown so she wouldn't have to see the moon through the window, low on the horizon, almost full and impossible to miss. Mallory pillowed her head on the small of Niua's back and flung her arms loosely around her. Niua loved Mallory's comforting weight, loved the feeling that they belonged together. She didn't want to sleep; she wanted to revel in their closeness, shut the curtains, and forget about the moon.

Soon, Mallory rolled off her and ran a hand up her leg in a question she needed no words to understand.

Niua turned regretfully onto her side. "I know it's not quite our last night together, but the moon is pulling at me, I can feel it, and it feels like goodbye. And I don't know how to have goodbye sex. Not with you."

"It's not goodbye. It won't be. Not tonight. Not tomorrow night. Not ever."

"It has to be." Niua propped herself up on one elbow. "I can't ask you to wait eighteen years for me."

"I don't plan to wait. I plan to *be* with you. Every day. No matter what you look like. Because you'll still be *you*. Your mind, your heart, your soul...those won't change."

Niua melted at that. "I love you, sea bean, but—"

"We'll meet at the beach every morning, before dawn, before anyone else is around. Or I'll get a sailboat and find you out in the ocean. We'll talk." Mallory tangled their feet together. "Even if we can't be together all the time, I want you to have someone you can count on, who loves you, who will be here when you return. I know you're used to your solitary existence, and maybe you like it, but if you want me to, I want to be the person who makes you feel less alone."

"That's really—" Really *what*, though? What was it? Wonderful? Optimistic? Impossible?

It was tempting to try to imagine a life together. But what kind of life would they have? They'd never be able to share a home or a bed. They'd never be able to go anywhere—or do anything—in public. Mallory would never be able to introduce Niua to her friends. If Mallory was injured, Niua would not be able to help. When Mallory grew old, Niua would not be at her side. Even if Mallory lived near a beach or on a boat, Niua would never be part of her world.

Eventually, Mallory would grow to resent her.

Better to end it now.

Niua couldn't meet her eyes. If Mallory refused to protect herself, then Niua would do it for her. No matter how much Niua wanted to beg her to stay, to say Yes, *please visit me every day for the rest of your life and I'll gladly swim in this bay until you get tired of me*, she wouldn't. For Mallory's sake. To not tie her to someone who could never be a real partner to her.

Mallory read her silence and let out a small, rough sob. "Don't do this. Don't give up on us before we've even tried."

Niua swallowed a lump in her throat. "It wouldn't be enough. For either of us."

Mallory deflated. Her whole body seemed to shut down. "I understand."

Winning felt terrible.

"You'd be bored," Mallory said, "being stuck in one place keeping me company when you could be exploring the world."

Never. But if it helped to let her think that, she wouldn't correct her. "I wish things could be different."

"So do I." Mallory wiped a tear off her face and sat up against the headboard. "I want to be angry at you. But I can't. I can't even run away and feel sorry for myself because I know this is our last chance to spend time together. And also because I'm pretty sure you don't want to end this any more than I do." She paused like she was hoping Niua would jump in and say she hadn't meant any of it and she couldn't wait to move in with her.

Wordlessly, Niua kissed away a fresh tear from Mallory's cheek.

Mallory heaved a sigh of resignation. "Come here," she said, patting her lap and stretching her legs out to make room.

Niua arranged herself between her legs, with her back to Mallory's front. Mallory ran her fingers through Niua's hair in a sensual sweep from her forehead to the top of her scalp to the nape of her neck. She retrieved her wide-tooth comb from the nightstand and pushed through her hair again, patiently smoothing out the tangles. When the tangles were gone, she continued, sweep after affectionate sweep. It was peaceful. Comforting. Safe. Niua slumped into the shelter of Mallory's body and curled into her.

Eventually, Mallory set the comb down. She pressed a kiss behind her ear and gathered Niua's hair in her hands. She gave her head another kiss. She divided her hair into sections and braided it flat along the side of her head, dropping kisses into the weave as she went.

Holding the end of the braid, Mallory brought it forward to show her. "I don't have a hair tie."

Niua pressed her hands to her hair—to the strands Mallory was holding and to those she couldn't see. She felt the braid's shape and imagined she could feel the warmth of Mallory's fingers lingering there. "I'll remember you forever."

"That doesn't help." Another kiss. "Ready for me to let go?"

Was she?

With one last kiss, Mallory released the ends, and her hair tumbled free.

30

The quay where Niua and Mallory disembarked the next morning was at the other end of the island from where the diary had been found. According to a pair of locals chatting by the water, the only person on the island who had a vehicle and could give them a ride was helping to repair a neighbor's roof and would return when he was finished. No, they couldn't say when that might be. There was a bench in the shade by the dirt road where they could wait.

"I'd rather walk than wait," Niua told Mallory.

Mallory checked the map. "It would take us several hours to reach the house on foot."

"I can do it if you can." She hadn't tripped over her feet in ages. It would be fine. Her body hummed with excitement. "I'm too impatient to sit."

"Yeah, no, for sure. I'm antsy, too."

Telling Mallory the truth about what she was searching for had been the right decision. Mallory understood there was no time to waste, and she'd been nothing but supportive. She'd obtained what they needed and made things happen, and done it all astonishingly fast. It was disappointing they hadn't found the wreck, but they'd done good work. She'd loved having Mallory at her side, sharing her thoughts, making the task feel more manageable.

She didn't know if coming here and seeing this island for herself would accomplish much, but she could continue her undersea search forever. These last days and hours were her final chance—for another eighteen years—to explore on land.

Mallory adjusted the straps on her small knapsack which held food and water, and off they went, side by side, in companionable silence. They passed a handful of opulent, weathered houses and a few shacks, but didn't encounter a soul. Niua picked up a fallen coconut from the base of a palm tree and tossed it from one hand to the other as she walked. Palm fronds swayed in the swirling gusts of an ocean breeze with a sound that was its own kind of music. When trees danced in the wind, did they feel joy? Did they feel free? Did they feel the same lightheartedness she did when she twirled underwater?

Her sense of jittery excitement increased. She could almost hear it, as if it was vibrating outside of her, like the sun prickling her skin, like waves crashing on the shore, like…

Like…

She gasped. The coconut in her hand dropped to the ground. It had been so long.

"I hear it."

"Hear what?" Mallory said.

The chanting of ancient voices.

The drizzle of raindrops splattering on the surface of the ocean.

The rush of a waterfall cascading down a cliff.

The crack of thawing sea ice.

The roar of the wind spiraling inside a cyclone.

The eerie echo of whales calling out to each other across the vastness of the deep.

The chalice's song.

What did Niua hear? A car? An animal? Those sorts of things wouldn't make her stop in the road—or tremble and stare blankly into the distance.

"Are you all right? Is it the heat?" Mallory uncapped her water and offered it to her.

Niua ignored it.

"Niua?"

"It's singing," she said in a hushed voice filled with awe.

Mallory gaped. No way. After all those days at sea, all those hours of Niua listening for a melody Mallory wouldn't be able to detect, all that disappointment. "The chalice?"

Niua nodded.

Of course shipwrecks were often found close to shore, but no one had believed this one would be. According to the diary, according to the wreck's lone survivor, it should be much farther out. For it to be *here*...

They should be shrieking with joy. Instead, Niua looked like she was in a trance, and Mallory was too stunned to do anything. Mallory tried to put the cap back on her water bottle, but she couldn't line up the threads. She'd fantasized that she'd be able to hear the song herself, that Niua had been wrong about that. But Niua was right. All she heard was the wind.

"Where is the sound coming from? Can you tell the direction?"

"Down this road. The direction we're going."

"Should we turn back and get the boat?"

"No. It's close. It makes more sense to continue walking until I know where the song is loudest. Then I can determine which side of the ocean it's coming from. Swim from there." Because unlike Mallory, no matter how far from shore the wreck was located, Niua didn't need a boat to reach it.

Mallory would have liked to be there at the final moment. To dive the wreck together. To not be left behind. She pulled Niua into a hug, their chins on each other's shoulders, so Niua wouldn't see if her face betrayed her. The only thing she wanted her to know was how thrilled she was for her.

"You did it," Mallory said.

Niua gave her a happy squeeze. "We did it."

Niua updated Mallory every few minutes. Mallory suspected Niua wanted to update her every few seconds but was restraining herself.

"Louder."

"Closer."

"We're heading in the right direction."

Two hours later, they reached the house that Adam Hollingshead had marked on their map with a star. The kidney-bean-shaped island narrowed here, granting oceanfront views to both the front and the back of the house. It was easy for Mallory to imagine someone at a second-story window or on the wraparound porch watching the *Ioanna* founder on the horizon.

The house wasn't their goal anymore—the source of the song was—so they continued on. A crumbling stone wall ran alongside the road, marking the edge of an extensive property. Near the end of it, Niua stopped. She cocked her head the way people did when a conversation didn't make sense and they were trying to decide if they'd misheard.

Mallory stopped beside her. "What is it?"

"I'm not sure." Niua pivoted and stalked back the way they'd come. She must have passed the loudest point and was tracking it down.

Mallory hurried after her. "Is this it? Are you leaving for the ocean now?"

"Not yet." Niua crossed the road, moving away from the diarist's home and toward another distant house, Mallory at her heels.

Niua meandered among the palm trees and across scraggly grass, zigzagging like she couldn't remember where she'd lost her sunglasses. Which made sense, because sounds could be tricky to track; it wasn't always obvious where they were coming from. After several minutes, Niua rubbed thoughtfully behind her ears. She turned back to the road, crossed to the low wall they'd followed earlier, and clambered over it.

Mallory balked. She'd just trespassed through someone else's land, but going over a wall felt more egregious than just crossing onto weedy sand. The house was quite some distance from the road, but still. "We can reach the beach just as easily by going around."

Niua reached over the wall and clasped Mallory's hand. "Come on. I don't think it's in the water. I think it's here."

"Inside the house?"

"Perhaps."

Mallory allowed her to lead her over the wall. "You think the pirate who survived took the chalice with him as his ship sank?"

"No. It would have been a struggle not to drown. He couldn't possibly have carried anything with him."

"Then how could the chalice be here?"

"Lots of things wash ashore: Seashells. Driftwood. Seaweed. Dead fish. Wine bottles. Plastic bags. Old coins from disintegrating shipwrecks—"

"Yeah, but..."

Niua started zigzagging again, pulling Mallory along with her and heading obliquely toward to the house. "The ocean brought the pirate here. Those same currents could have brought all sorts of other interesting things along the same path to the same place."

The pirate would have known what loot the ship held. He could have watched the shore for treasure. Had he been lucky enough to find it?

"I guess it doesn't matter how it got here," Mallory said. The only thing that mattered was finding it. "So we'll go see if anyone's home?"

Niua didn't reply. Judging by the intense look of concentration on her face, she may not have even heard her. Silently, she spun around in place like a compass needle confounded by the pull of a magnet that was too close.

Mallory stepped back to give her space.

Niua slowed, then stopped. "Stay here," she commanded. Then added, more gently, "Please."

And ran off.

This wasn't anything like the last time Niua left her behind—the circumstances were different, and Mallory was confident she'd return—but it was hard not to chase after her. And wait. And trust that although Niua *would* abandon her soon, it wasn't going to be now.

Mallory chewed the inside of her cheek until she tasted blood. When Niua returned, she was carrying a shovel over her shoulder.

"Where'd *that* come from?"

"There was a garden shed beside that other house." Niua indicated the direction of the road with a tilt of her head. "I noticed it when we were over there."

"You can't just..." Mallory sputtered. She'd never thought of herself as a rule follower, but clearly she very much was.

"I already did."

"Does this mean it's buried?" She glanced at the ground—at the spot where Niua had asked her to stay put. Was she standing over buried treasure?

Niua planted the shovel blade into the ground with enough force that it stuck. "It does."

"That's—"

"Beautiful day, isn't it, ladies?" bellowed a voice from a distance. It was far, but not that far. Not far away enough.

They both startled. Niua lost her balance and knocked into the shovel's handle. She fumbled with it, then closed her grip around it and steadied herself.

Outside the front door of the house—the house whose property they were about to dig on without permission—stood a man holding a rifle. He was pointing it at the ground, but it wasn't exactly a friendly pose.

Mallory's heart pounded like the crashing surf during a storm.

"I'm afraid I'm going to have to ask you to leave and stick to the road. This is private property."

"Oh," Mallory said ineloquently. Her head felt like it was floating precariously on her spine. The best thing would be to turn and walk away, but she couldn't move. Adam had mentioned the person who lived here was a recluse with a temper. He hadn't said anything about him being a threat.

"I'll take care of this," Niua said calmly, smoothing her hair with one hand and arranging it around her shoulders while holding the shovel at a jaunty angle that suggested a tap dancer's cane.

"What? No!" Mallory rasped, snapping out of her paralysis and hoping the man couldn't hear her. "He's not going to respond to you sucking on your hair. It's not safe."

"I need to get closer," Niua said under her breath.

"That does not sound like a good idea."

"I need to make eye contact."

"He can already see you."

Niua ignored her and called out to the man. "Hello! What a lovely home you have."

The man raised his rifle a few degrees, not pointing it directly at them, but clearly not bound by the same standards of reasonable behavior that most people followed. "Thank you. Now move along."

Niua just stood there. Mallory did, too, because she was about to faint.

Niua eyed her assessingly. Mallory had the disconcerting feeling she was being judged a liability. "You should stay back."

"So I can escape to safety while you face him on your own? No."

"I'll be fine."

Mallory glared at her. "You said you're not immortal."

"The chalice is here," Niua hissed, barely audible. "I'm not leaving."

"We can come back for it."

"He's not going to hurt two silly, ignorant women. He's merely trying to scare us."

"Yes, well, he succeeded."

"I'm going to go over there and talk to him. I need to be closer for the magic to take hold."

Magic.

How had she watched Niua win over everyone in her path and not realized?

She'd thought her flirting was the reason men fell all over her. Incredibly effective, unmagical, human flirting.

She hadn't understood the flirting was a cover. It hadn't occurred to her that Niua used it to lure men into range, and then, as an additional benefit, any onlookers who weren't under her spell had a plausible explanation for the men's behavior.

Not that anyone would actually believe she was wielding magic.

So. Okay. Magic would take care of this guy. But not if it didn't work at a distance.

"You can really convince him to let us dig? Put his rifle down and offer us iced tea?"

"I'll convince him to leave. He won't have any idea what we're doing."

"Not until he returns and sees a hole in the ground."

"At that point, he'll be too busy nursing a headache to notice."

More puzzle pieces clicked into place. "Like the men on the *Sea Monster*. The headaches are an aftereffect of what you do to them."

Mallory searched her memories. Had she herself had a headache at any point since she'd met Niua? Could she have been oblivious while Niua manipulated her?

No. No headaches. And those first few days with her on the ship, Mallory had been the only person who *hadn't* reacted to her like an enamored idiot.

She might be in love with her now, but it hadn't been instantaneous.

And then Niua had refused to charter a fishing boat captained by a female…

Because her magic worked only on men.

It seemed so obvious now. And what the pattern revealed was a power that was not a guarantee, a rule founded on a muddled boundary.

"Are you sure your magic will work on him?"

"Weren't you the one who told me certainty was boring?"

"Did you hear me?" the man said. "If you ladies are done chitchatting—"

"Hey," Niua called out, interrupting him. "You're the reason none of the fishermen on the other islands know about the history of this house or the probable location of the *Ioanna*, aren't you?"

Fishermen? What was she talking about?

His expression turned stormier. "What do you know about this house?"

Strolling oh-so-casually toward him, her eyes fixed on his, Niua slid her hand along the shaft of the shovel. Mallory would have rolled her eyes and laughed at the crassness of it if she weren't so worried.

"You value your privacy," Niua said. "You don't want nosy tourists trespassing on your property." She continued steadily forward. The thing with the shovel seemed to be working. "You don't want shipwreck hunters pestering you with questions. Knocking on your door. Looking in your windows. Taking photos."

How close did Niua have to get? If her magic didn't kick in soon, what would happen? Mallory dug her nails into her palms. She wanted to believe in her, but it was asking a lot.

"You made sure none of the islanders found out where the diary came from."

The man cracked a smile that oozed superiority. "The islanders don't care about finding the *Ioanna*. They want the tourists to believe whatever they tell them. They want to lead them to the wrecks they already know about that are easy to dive and that look like the wrecks they show in movies."

"Understandably." Niua was directly in front of him now.

The man lowered his rifle. "I don't get many intruders coming around here anymore."

"I'm glad to hear that."

"Hasn't always been the case." His posture and his tone were more relaxed now. Anyone who didn't know better would think he was catching up with an old friend.

Mallory unclenched her fists.

"I noticed quite a few tourists anchored at the other end of the island," Niua lied with a note of concern. "I think you'd be able to head them off if you went down there as soon as possible."

"As soon as possible," he agreed, and walked away toward the road. Just like that. Like it was his own idea.

Mallory was embarrassed she'd ever believed mere flirting could explain *that.*

It didn't take long to dig a hole. The soil was sandy, and Niua knew exactly where to aim. They spotted the first hint of metal sooner than Mallory'd expected, not nearly as deep as she'd imagined. Niua cautiously loosened the soil in a circle around it, then set the shovel down and dug with her hands. Mallory shrugged out of her knapsack and let it drop to the ground. She knelt beside her and pushed the accumulating pile of soil out of the way.

And there it was. Not even in a box, just...there. Niua gave a strangled squeak and covered her mouth like she could prevent her emotions from escaping. Trembling, she freed the chalice and lifted it out of the ground. She rubbed at the dirt that clung to it. It didn't look like much, its details hidden under decades of dirt, but the reverence with which Niua pressed her lips to its curved surface was breathtaking. It was a private moment, a victory only Niua truly understood. But Mallory felt like she was part of it, too.

Niua held the chalice to her heart, hugging it. "I won't have to carry the weight of memory by myself anymore," she whispered, relief cracking through her words. There were tear tracks on her cheeks. "I won't be the end of the line. I won't be alone."

31

"You won't be the end of the line?" Mallory echoed quietly. Dangerously. "What does that mean?"

Niua swore under her breath. She'd developed a terrible habit of relaxing her vigilance around Mallory and saying things that were better left unsaid.

Mallory edged away. "I think I know what it means." One slip, but it was enough to lead her to its logical conclusion. Mallory scooted back until she was sitting on the opposite side of the ground they'd torn up. "Why didn't you tell me?"

I've never told anyone. Mallory'd never asked what the chalice was used for, and Niua was accustomed to keeping secrets. There'd been no reason to tell her, not when she didn't have the chalice. But now…

"Why didn't I tell you that the chalice allows me to transform women into memory keepers?" That it linked her to her sisters and to the lineage of memory keepers, to those in the past and to those in the future? That it allowed her to call to the goddess who dreamed in the ocean's depths? That through that connection, the goddess could manifest her own kaleidoscopic nature in others? And create shapeshifters? Until once again there were nine?

"Mermaids," Mallory clarified.

"Yes."

"You could turn me into a mermaid."

"I'm not going to do that."

"Why not?" Mallory protested. "You're going to turn *someone* into a mermaid. I know you are. Why can't it be me? I want this. I want to be the one."

Niua wanted it, too. But it would be selfish of her to take her away from everything Mallory had ever known. "You don't know what you're asking. To give up your whole world? Your whole life? It will change you in ways you won't expect. You can't possibly—"

"I love the unknown. It's what I love about being a scientist. Getting to explore a mysterious new world is the best future I can imagine."

"You say that now." Niua tightened her grip on the chalice. "You could take a few days to think it over. A few months, even. We can turn you anytime."

"How long did *you* have to think about it before *you* decided?"

"That was different. Barbarians were shooting arrows at us. It was life or death. There was no time."

"You didn't even get to choose, did you?" Mallory said, her voice gentling. "Your goddess made the choice for you."

"No. That's not…" That day was seared into her memory so vividly. "All right, yes, it was the goddess's decision, but I'd already agreed to devote my life to her."

"Which you did without knowing what that commitment would require of you."

"I would have said yes. If she'd asked. I was happy to do what she needed."

"But it's *not* okay for *me* to commit without knowing what the future holds?"

"I don't want you to do something you'll regret and won't be able to undo."

"I'm willing to take that risk. Every decision we ever make is a potential mistake. We jump in blindly no matter how prepared we think we are. It shouldn't stop us from making them."

Mallory crowded the edge of the hole in the ground and reached for her, bridging the distance between them. Niua hesitated, but took her hand. Mallory had seemed so cynical and suspicious when they first met, but it had been hiding this deep well of optimism.

"You're protecting me," Mallory said. "And I love that you want to do that, but you don't have to." She interlaced their fingers. "You abandoned a life you loved. Because you were in danger. But my life is different. It never fit. If I do this, it won't be to hide. I'm not running away. I'm running *toward*. Toward a new life. Toward a new world. Toward you."

Niua's heart filled with a sea of stars, each one a burst of joy. "Yeah, I..." She was the tide, ready to turn. Energy, rising, surging. "Yeah. I want that, too."

32

Mallory wasn't used to being protected—she'd sworn off any desire to be shielded from difficult choices when she'd escaped the well-meaning, suffocating protectiveness of her parents—but she understood why Niua was worried. It was sweet, really, that Niua loved her so much that she'd push her away.

Infuriating.

But sweet.

Caring.

Enough to turn her heart to mush.

Now that Niua had said yes.

Mallory thrummed with excitement. "What happens next?"

On a desolate white sand beach not far from where they'd found the chalice, Mallory scrawled a note to her parents and another one to her boss. Her friends...well...there wasn't anyone who would immediately notice she was gone. As Adam had warned, her phone was useless out here, so this was the best she could do.

"Will your family search for you?" Niua asked.

"I'm telling everyone I'm doing research on a remote island and won't be in contact with civilization for several years."

"If you want to wait and say goodbye in person—"

"I don't." There wasn't anyone she wanted to drag this out for. And if she found herself missing anyone later on, she could always sweet-talk a sailor into letting her borrow his satellite phone.

Niua wandered along the shore disentangling trash from

beached seaweed while she waited for Mallory to finish.

Mallory tucked the letters into her knapsack and planted it in the sand above the high tide line, which felt like a better choice than leaving her belongings at the door of a man who hated trespassers.

Niua returned with an empty wine bottle. "Use this. A message in a bottle will be more fun for whoever finds it, so they'll be more likely to have your letters delivered."

Mallory rolled up her notes and slid them inside the bottle. She stuck the bottle in the sand beside her knapsack and stoppered it with the cork Niua handed her.

"You'll need to remove your..." Niua gestured toward Mallory's trousers.

Mallory stripped off her clothes.

As Niua joined in and pulled her own dress off over her head, a piece of paper fluttered out of her pocket. The map of the island. A gust of wind caught it and pushed it toward Mallory's knees. Sharp grains of sand hit her shins. The wind twirled the map out of reach and blew it away.

At the mutable boundary between land and sea, her feet sinking into the sand, Mallory waded into the swell until she was waist-deep.

Niua placed the chalice full of seawater in Mallory's hands. Together, they raised the chalice overhead, toward the heavens. Water sloshed over the edges. Niua sang a long, clear note.

Images flashed through Mallory's mind: women singing in the forest, being shot at by arrows, escaping into the sea.

Voices spoke in a language she'd never heard, yet understood.

In the beginning, a tear was rent in the fabric of reality.

The tear became a rift.

The rift expanded until it was no longer perceived as a rift at all.

Mallory imagined diving into the abyss. Her thighs tingled. Her blood was fizzy with anticipation.

More images came to her: Mermaids swimming in the ocean's great currents, exploring the tunnels of a sea cave, hiding the chalice in a crevice in the rock. Strangers in dugout canoes, longships, barques, schooners, galleons, steamboats, ocean liners, aircraft carriers, submarines...

Sudden cramping seized her pelvis. The small of her back arched. Her body was no longer under her control.

She is everything.

She is nothing.

She is neither.

She is both.

She is.

Is.

She is waiting to be remembered.

She is waiting to return.

She will loosen the fabric of reality. Again.

The cramps faded away.

Mallory lost her footing and fell with a splash.

She kicked her way to the surface—with her tail—and let out a whoop of joy. She flung her arms around Niua. They'd done it.

She was mer.

The sea was waiting.

EPILOGUE

Niua relaxed on a boulder on an uncharted beach among hundreds of seals sunning themselves into a stupor. Mallory's head was in Niua's lap, their tails entwined.

Five other mermaids lounged nearby, their long hair obscuring their bare chests, their tails blending in with the seals'.

Ju-Fen was drilling them on the finer points of Chinese grammar while Niua wove a straw sunhat out of long strands of beach grass, occasionally setting it on the ground to stroke Mallory's hair.

In time, there would be nine of them. They'd never replace her lost sisters, but these young mermaids would carry on her tribe's legacy.

"When are you going to teach us more about ocean currents?" Mallory whispered to her.

"Pay attention to your new sister," Niua whispered back.

"I'd rather pay attention to you." Mallory nuzzled into Niua's waist.

Niua lost track of everything but her.

Later, Mallory and Niua visited a beach populated by people rather than seals. While Mallory bobbed in the gentle waves near shore, carrying on an animated conversation with another swimmer, Niua lurked underwater nearby, watching, making sure Mallory was safe.

It was risky, but Mallory couldn't resist the lure of keeping up with the latest scientific highlights and was a master at not getting caught. In a scavenged bikini top, her tail hidden beneath the murky water, Mallory looked every bit the vacationing beachgoer.

Afterward, they slipped away underwater without attracting attention. When they surfaced a kilometer away, Mallory was bursting with excitement. "He said the tsunami we saw hit New Zealand was triggered by an undersea volcanic eruption, not an earthquake. No one knows if it was because of the energy of the explosion or if the flank collapsed, which would have displaced massive amounts of water. Want to go see?" She looked so happy. She'd embraced her new life with an enthusiasm that made Niua forget she'd ever worried whether Mallory would adapt.

"Of course."

"It's going to be amazing."

Mallory loved visiting regions of the ocean that scientists could only dream of. There was always something new to explore. And Niua couldn't think of anything more perfect than doing it with her.

ABOUT THE AUTHOR

Siri Caldwell does not believe in waiting for frogs to turn into princesses, because frogs are cute the way they are. Her novella *Mistletoe Mishap* was a Lambda Literary Award finalist.

Visit her online at www.siricaldwell.com